a novel

BRAIN STORM

A. M. WILHELM

Acknowledgments

The list of people who have brought this book into creation is long. You know who you are. This work, in fact no work, is created in isolation. As all novels are, it was simultaneously an individual and collective effort. Thank you for caring enough to make *Brainstorm* a creation I can feel proud of.

Page design by Cliff Snyder

Cover design by Dejan Djordjevic

Brainstorm

ISBN: 9781070316772

Dedicated to my past,

present, and future readers.

Without you, books like this one

would lose their purpose.

You are essential.

You are appreciated.

CONTENTS

CHAPTER 1

DARK SIDE

An involuntary growl escaped Nick Sperry's throat. What the hell was the director of the National Institutes of Health doing at an orphanage? He tracked the man's movement until the guy turned the street corner, vanishing out of sight.

Pulling his ubiquitous pad and pen out of his chest pocket, he wrote, *Connection between Warner and Sunshine Children's Home, D.C.?* He closed the pad and secured it in his pocket.

His girlfriend exited the building fifteen minutes after Warner. Her mouth was tight, the sparkle in her pale blue eyes flat-lined. As she approached the car, Nick went around to the passenger side to open her door. She dropped into the seat without making eye contact. She buckled up and looked down, a cascade of dark hair shielding her face from view.

Nick got back into the car and placed a hand on her leg. "Baby, what happened?"

"They had no record of him." Nick had to lean in to hear her.

"What?"

"I don't want to talk about it."

"Melissa, please."

"Nick…" She turned to face him, her features disconcertingly blank. "I can't. I'm sorry."

Knowing her well, Nick responded with a nod and started the engine to head for home.

No record of a friggin' child? What the hell had they done with Sidney? It was a difficult thing to ignore, especially when Warner might be involved. But Nick didn't push. Getting Melissa to talk when she didn't want to was like trying to get your fingers out of Chinese handcuffs. The more you tugged, the worse things went.

"Damn it!" Nick swore. "Jesus, that was hot!" He slammed the mug down on the black granite counter then watched as the droplets of coffee flung outward, narrowly missing the cuff of his white button-down. The shower of liquid and its near miss were a warning. The sprays of errant coffee hadn't caught him, but Melissa might. He let out a loud sigh. He was only doing what he thought was best for her, what he knew she wouldn't be able to do for herself.

Nick sponged away the reminder of his dishonesty. Then, with the precision of a slap shot, he flung the sponge into the sink. It hit the side and fell dead. He leaned one hand against the dark granite, snatched his phone out of his pocket, and tapped a contact number.

"Hi, is this Ms. Malcolm?"

"This is she. Mr. Sperry? That's you, right?" She didn't wait for his response. She sounded excited, like a puppy with a new toy. "I'm so glad you called. Can you come over today? I need to show you something.

It might be a clue. And I have some more thoughts about the potential culprit. And—"

"Ms. Malcolm, I won't be able to take your case."

She continued, undeterred. "I was also thinking that—"

Nick stifled a sigh. "Ms. Malcolm, I won't be able to help you."

"What? What do you mean?"

"Something's come up."

Ms. Malcolm's voice went from alto to soprano. "But… the retainer I gave you?"

"Will be returned to you today."

"But…" The word sounded brittle.

"I'm sorry, Ms. Malcolm."

He heard an exaggerated "humph" and the sound of Ms. Malcolm slamming down her phone.

Good riddance. He and Melissa didn't need the income from his PI work because Melissa's real estate career was lucrative. Still, Nick wasn't going to become some kind of kept man. He had balls between his legs. He blew out a long breath. The investigation for Sidney was important. He would forgo a couple of jobs while he searched for him.

Nick peered down into his cup and saw trace semicircles of coffee etched into the bottom, signaling his memory lapse. He couldn't remember drinking the rest. *Not acceptable.*

His pounding steps echoed down the hall and into the bedroom. Arms crossed over his chest, Nick surveyed the line of suits in his closet. Then reached for one an employee with a low-paying government job would wear—visual collateral that he was from the Department of Children and Families or DCF. It wouldn't be hard to fool them. Nick was an expert in deceit, although he didn't take any pride in it.

He drove his S6 to Sunshine Children's Home and found the same parking spot, almost right in front. He frowned. It was a strange coincidence. And, he didn't believe in coincidences. He halfway expected to find Sebastian Warner walking out of Sunshine. His expression steeled, if that asshole appeared again he would chase him down. Extract some answers.

Jumping out of the car and into the street, a horn blared and tires skidded as the driver of a silver BMW braked hard, swerving to avoid him. "Watch where you're going!" Nick yelled at the rear of the car. He slammed his car door shut, taking one large step over the curb. Rolling his shoulders backward a couple times, he worked the irritation out of his body to get into character.

There were those ridiculous yellow walls, and large, freshly washed windows blaring like a beacon. Instinctively, he rehearsed how he'd tell Mel he lied to her if there wasn't any good news to soften the blow. The scenario wasn't promising. *Screw it!* He'd made his decision. Second-guessing was death.

"Sir?"

Nick blinked and looked over at the woman who spoke. She was about five feet tall, her graying hair held in a tight bun, and she wore an inexpensive trench coat. Based on these data points, and, given her proximity to the building, Nick presumed she worked at the children's home.

The woman flicked her chin in the direction of Sunshine. "Going inside?"

Nick followed her gaze. "As a matter of fact, I am."

Nick could almost see the string of questions hidden in the lines of her brow.

"I could see you standing here from blocks away. You didn't move for minutes."

Nick stared at her, declining to answer.

She tilted her head sideways, pursing her lips as she gave him a head-to-toe assessment. "Are you looking to adopt or foster?"

Nick changed his cover story on the spot. "Well…" He drew in a deep breath as he contemplated the pavement. "I just found out a woman I dated eight years ago left my son here. She didn't tell me about him until a few weeks ago. We broke up before I knew she was pregnant. Anyway…" He leveled his eyes with hers. "I want to know what happened to him."

The woman regarded Nick but he couldn't read her expression, which was rare. She held out a hand. "I'm Dorothy Williams, program coordinator here at Sunshine." They shook. "Come inside. We'll see what I can find out for you."

Nick followed her plain black boots up the cement steps. At the door, he reached for the handle. "Allow me." She looked surprised by the gesture. Nick pulled the door open and waved her in before him.

"Thank you," Williams said as she entered. "Hi, Janet," she greeted a younger woman sitting behind a desk located in the front foyer. Ms. Williams turned and said, "Follow me."

The decor in the fifteen by fifteen-foot office matched Sunshine's exterior—a little too pretty, almost saccharine-sweet, like an old aunt's living room. Williams motioned to one of three puffy, rose-colored chairs arranged in a triangle. "Sit down."

Nick unbuttoned his suit jacket and sank down into the plush chair. He felt like he was being sucked into a giant marshmallow. Shifting his position, he moved to the edge of the cushion. That was a little better.

Williams hung her coat on a rack and retrieved a pen and pad from the desk. Eyeing Nick, she sat across from him in one of the oversized armchairs. Positioning her pen above the paper, she asked, "What child are you looking for?"

Nick wrung his hands while he studied a coffee-colored stain on the ivory carpet, trying to imagine what a real father would feel like in his position. "Sidney Ryder."

He watched from beneath his eyelids as the pen fell from William's grip, its point piercing the page like a dart. Her face tightened then relaxed a second later. Nick suspected she was more intelligent, and her job more important, than she wanted him to guess.

In a cool, measured tone, she replied, "A woman came by here a few days ago asking about that child. I told her there was no record of him. I was quite clear about it, though she refused to believe me." She brought her chin down sharply to indicate that as far as she was concerned, the matter was closed.

Nick glanced down at her boots. As he noticed before, they were worn down on the outside edge, indicating a distinct turnout. Maybe she had been a ballerina in her younger years. That might explain her bun, too—could be another remnant of her past. Nick released a breath—his observations were likely irrelevant. He brought his eyes up. "She didn't tell me that."

Williams placed the pad on a small table beside her chair and laid the pen on top with strained exactness, as though the placement of a writing utensil could decide the fate of the world. She clasped her hands, bringing them to rest on her lap, then leaned toward Nick. "Have you considered that she, um, might have forgotten where she took her baby?" She smiled with no sympathy in her eyes. "Many mothers are not in their right minds when they come here ... drugs, alcohol ..." She let the words dangle between them.

It was his natural instinct to defend Melissa and in a single instant, Nick had to harness every bit of his professional training. He barely succeeded. "No, ma'am," he replied. He made sure he pronounced ma'am so that it sounded like an insult. "I hadn't thought of that."

Williams persisted with her false grin. "Well, as I told your girlfriend—"

Nick interjected, "Ex-girlfriend."

She brought a fist up to her mouth to cover a fake cough. "Yes, as I told your ex-girlfriend, that child never came to Sunshine. I'll leave it up to you to fill in the blanks." She moved her lips in a way that approximated a smile but wasn't. It was clearly either an accusation or a warning.

Nick rose from his seat so his broad-shouldered six-foot six frame would tower over her. "Thank you for the information." The smile he offered was just like hers, a social exchange of insincerity.

Striding past the girl at the desk, he exited Sunshine. As soon as he got in his car, he made a call.

"What's up, Nick?" came the reply through the Audi's speakers.

"Hey, Sam. I need a favor."

Sam Prezziato snickered. "Isn't that the only reason you ever call me? Or did you want to meet for some tea and crumpets? We can talk about the queen if you like. What do we think about her new violet-colored hat?" He paused dramatically to allow time for his wit to be admired, then added, in a more jovial tone, "What the hell do you want, Mr. CIA?"

Nick pulled into the street and turned the corner, frowning as he encountered heavy traffic. "I need to hire Mr. H to access some files. They'll probably be encrypted." As he spoke he took a hard right down a side street, confident he could drive around the jam. A small pulse of satisfaction made him relax his grip on the wheel, as he saw the clear road ahead.

Nick could almost hear the smirk as Sam replied, "Oh, you want Mr. H, huh? He's a busy man. I don't have to tell you he ain't cheap."

Mr. H was the best hacker in Sam's network, meriting the extra expense. "I know what you charge for him. I'm willing to pay."

Sam let silence loiter around for several seconds. "Did you know that the fee recently went up for his illustrious services? He's in very high demand. Is it a rush job, or can you afford to wait?"

Nick sucked air through his teeth. Obviously, Sam was in the mood to play games. His temper got the better of him. "Jesus, Sam! I've been working with you for years. What the hell?"

The other end of the line went deathly silent.

Nick got his anger under control. "How about you grandfather me in at the old price?" He tried to sound lighthearted.

"Can't do that. I'm just a man trying to make an honest living. Can't be giving out freebies—slippery slope and all that." Sam actually believed that shit, and he didn't take very kindly to being contradicted. "Tell you what, Nick. I'll cut you a break because I like you so much."

Sam quoted a price that was still outrageous. Unfortunately, no one could change Sam Prezziato's mind once it was made up, so Nick agreed. He sped up unconsciously, thinking at least he didn't have to deal with traffic *and* Sam's bullshit at the same time.

"Okay, so now that we've gotten the unpleasantries out of the way..." Sam chuckled.

Nick wasn't quite ready to let go of his annoyance. "Really, Sam?"

Sam laughed heartily. "Hey, come on, it was a good joke. You gotta give it to me."

Nick relented. "Fine. It was a good joke." He ended with a half-laugh to show that things were fine between them which, actually, they were. Sam could be an ass, but he wasn't mean-spirited. In fact, Nick liked him, at least, he did most of the time. He was a difficult person, but he had a good heart. Nick had seen the evidence of it on a few memorable occasions.

"What do you need Mr. H to get for you?"

Nick gave Sam the specifics.

"A flash drive with the downloaded files will take a day or two," Sam explained. "It will be done by Wednesday, for sure. We could meet for lunch, my treat."

Nick smiled. Only Sam could demonstrate his cheapness and his generosity in the course of a conversation lasting a few minutes. "Okay. How about we meet at two on Wednesday?"

"Sure, two, at Café Dupont. And Nick..."

"Yeah, Sam?"

"You're welcome."

"Asshole," Nick said in a stage whisper and hung up.

CHAPTER 2

DEMONS

L ike a crying child on a rapidly descending plane, the smoke
detector wailed as though its life depended on it. *Little do you
know,* Nick thought as he stalked out of the pantry, broom in
hand, proceeding to whack the offending alarm. There was an undeclared
war between him and all smoke detectors, carbon monoxide detectors,
and other beeping indicators that inhabited his otherwise peaceful home.
The alarm broke loose from the ceiling, shattering into several pieces.

Undeterred by the fleeting nature of his triumph, Nick shouted at the
remnants, *I won, you little bastard.*

He used his weapon to sweep up the evidence then returned his attention to the garlic sizzling in the pan on the stovetop, a key ingredient
for his special Shrimp Fra Diavolo, Melissa's favorite. Butter was another
essential and would hopefully combine with his plans for the evening to
butter her up.

The sound of the garage door opening coincided with a desultory push of his spatula. She was home. Tension and excitement competed for control over his nervous system. Sorry excuse for an agent.

With the deftness of muscle memory, he switched his docked iPhone from playing his favorite sports talk radio show to a Coldplay album Melissa liked. Standing over the stove, he waved a hand over the frying pan, urging the scent upwards. The pungent odor of garlic filled his nostrils, forecasting an almost-ready dinner.

Click. Click. Click, came the sound of Melissa's heels across the terracotta tiles as she walked into the kitchen. "Hey, honey, didn't you text me earlier that I could have my favorite dessert first?" she teased. "But, by the smell, it seems like everything is almost ready." Pouting, she walked over to Nick and kissed him, letting her lips linger for a minute on his, betraying no trace of the distress he'd sensed in her just a few days ago.

Not wanting to destroy the mood, Nick let himself enjoy her. They could talk soon. "Hey, baby. I can keep everything warm in the oven."

Melissa pursed her lips as if in thought then giggled. "Actually, I am kind of hungry." She lifted her gaze to meet his own. "But you probably already knew that." She laughed again as she put down her bag, took off her coat, and continued chatting. "It is eight o'clock, after all."

Nick finished her sentence. "And we both know you always get hungry at eight, no matter what you say beforehand. But I'm the only one who ever seems to remember that important fact." He winked at her. "I know how to take care of you, Mel."

Her eyes twinkled, her nose twitching slightly. "You do." She paused. "Oh, before I forget, tomorrow night Victoria and I are going to do some sparring together at the gym, so I won't be home until late."

"Okay. Tell Vic I said hi. Feels like I haven't seen her in forever."

Nick eyed Melissa as she took off her shoes and put them next to the bar in the kitchen. She read his mind. and laughed. "Sorry baby, they hurt.

It's been a long day." She smiled at him. "As for Vic, she's been really busy, but it's good. She's going to close on that twelve-million-dollar property she's been working on this Saturday."

"That's great! Good for her." Nick filled their plates with pasta and shrimp.

Melissa took the plates from him and carried them to the table. Nick joined her and poured them both some of his favorite Italian wine, Amarone. So, how are you doing with that waterfront condo?"

Melissa gave a soft snort. "Oh, you mean the one BB is interested in?" She twirled a fork through the linguine and took a bite.

Nick raised his eyebrows. "BB?"

Melissa held a hand in front of her face while she finished chewing. She swallowed and answered, "Blonde Bitch." She reached for her glass.

Nick laughed. "But she's still interested?"

Melissa shifted her head in a side-to-side motion. "We'll see. She may just be playing with me."

"I'd like to play with you."

She swallowed a long draft of wine, looking at him over the rim of her glass. "You always do, NN." Her eyes flickered.

He put his glass down too forcefully. "Tell me what NN means. I can't think straight right now."

"Naughty Nick."

He grinned and nodded. "Of course."

Melissa rolled over in their king bed and nestled into the crook of Nick's arm. "Well, as I predicted, dessert was definitely my favorite course of the evening." She kissed him on the temple. "Although you do make a mean Fra Diavolo."

Nick squeezed her shoulder. "I have to be good for something around here now that you're pulling in the big bucks."

"You know I love my work. I'm just lucky at it, I guess." Melissa wriggled and cuddled up closer to him.

"You're good at it, baby. That's why you're successful. You've earned it. I'm so proud of you."

"I know you are." She paused and changed the subject, which she always did when Nick complimented her. "Hey, did you decide to take that weird case about the guy who keeps on breaking into his ex-wife's house just to steal her panties?"

Nick took in a quick breath and relaxed the muscles of his brow. "Oh, you must mean Ms. Malcolm's case. She actually doesn't really know who's breaking in. Might not be the ex. Could even be his new girlfriend."

"Wow, that would be even weirder. Who would do that?"

"There are a lot of strange people in the world, Melissa."

Melissa shrugged. "I guess. Anyway, did you take the case?"

Nick sat up in bed. Melissa kept her head on his chest as he rose, adjusting her body.

"I want to talk to you about that—"

Melissa interrupted. "Nick, you know I don't care if you work or not. I just like being with you. Money's money. It doesn't really matter. You've done a lot for me. I wouldn't mind if you let me return the favor now and again." She looked up at him.

"I know. I'm working on that." He held her closer and looked at her expectantly. He hoped she would understand that what he was about to say was important. "But this isn't about money. The reason I didn't take the job was because I wanted to have the time to help you look for Sidney. We should find out what happened to him. And I didn't want to worry you, but that day at the children's home, I saw—"

"Nick, I don't want to look for him, you know that." Her frown deepened. "You do know that ... Nick." Her enunciation converted his name to a reprimand.

Nick could see the rigidity travel through her muscles in a gathering surge from her tensed forehead downward.

"Did you think I was lying?" Melissa jerked away from him, yanking the sheet up to anchor it into her armpits until a tight band of white fabric constricted her chest. "I wasn't lying, Nick. I don't want to know. It seems you don't understand. You probably don't even believe me. Just remember. You. Aren't. Me."

As Nick reached a hand toward her, she made herself more compact. Only the sharp places of her body showed, everything soft she protected. Nick sighed. At the center of Melissa's cocoon of self-preservation was the decision she'd made eight years ago. Like a festering wound, it could only be healed if it was opened back up. He wanted to help her, but to do that he needed to lie to her again.

"Okay. I understand."

Melissa looked into his eyes, as though trying to see into his soul. Eventually, she stopped staring at him and settled back into the crook of his arm. Nick savored her surrender, tenuous though it was.

CHAPTER 3

ENCRYPTION

The valet took his keys. Another man in a dark suit opened the door to Maison Dupont. Nick saw Sam inside, to the left.

Nick chuckled to himself when he saw Sam's outfit, illustrating perfectly the inherent Italian-American love for fashion that flirts—sometimes overtly—with gaudiness. He was attired in one of his immaculate Armani suits paired with a purple Gucci shirt opened to the third button. Around his neck was a thick gold chain, and in his left hand he held his ever-present glass of single malt scotch.

Nick walked over to him and tapped him on the shoulder. "Hey, Sam," he said, and they shook hands. "Thanks for getting us reservations. I know it's impossible to get in here."

Sam shrugged. "No big deal."

"Not for someone with your connections."

Sam slanted his smile, taking a sip of scotch. "You could say that." He lifted up his drink. "Want one?"

"No, thanks. I'll wait."

"Suit yourself." Sam nodded and went to talk to the manager. As he spoke, his hands moved nonstop. Every inch of Prezziato embodied his Southern Italian heritage, including his demonstrative gestures. He also had dark, wavy hair, pitch-dark eyes, and tan skin to complete the look.

Nick wore a navy Brooks Brothers suit that was at least seven years old. His shirt was one Melissa had picked out. She had insisted it matched. Good enough for him.

Over cocktails and a leisurely lunch, they chatted about football, wine, and opera. Nick knew a lot about the first two subjects but very little about the third. Nick listened as Sam described the differences between Italian and German operas. Sam was smart and interesting, which counterbalanced his controlling side—usually.

"So which do you like better, German or Italian?"

Sam huffed out a breath and rested his glass of scotch on the table. With his eyes on the ceiling, he considered the question for a long moment. Finally, he twisted his lips into an expression that was half smile, half grimace. "Let me get back to you on that one."

"Difficult question?"

"More than you know." Sam lifted his napkin from his lap, folded it in thirds, then in thirds again. He placed it next to his plate with exactitude as if he was Picasso trying to determine his next brush stroke. "Anyway," he said, "on a different subject, Mr. H hinted that there was something pretty interesting about those files." Sam slipped a hand into his pocket and pulled out a flashdrive, handing it to Nick.

Nick secured it in his palm and raised his eyebrows, waiting for more information to be doled out. Whenever Sam knew something was important, he made Nick pay for it, once with cash and a second time with every store of patience he had.

Sam coughed, sitting back in his chair. "Turns out that when he was hacking into their system, he noticed some familiar security features."

Sam paused again, tapping his finger on the table in 4/4 time while Nick watched. In some kind of bizarre finale, he rapped his knuckles once against the table. The sound reverberated through the room and a few patrons looked around, startled. Sam leaned further back in his chair and locked his hands behind his head.

Nick concentrated on the triangular space created by Sam's arms. Focusing on the geometry of Sam's limbs became a mantra of tolerance. Time passed. Nick wasn't sure exactly how much.

"Their encoding system mimics the one the National Institutes of Health uses."

Nick's eyes broadened, then contracted. He thought of Warner. Then he noticed a tightness in Sam's lips. He held something back, Nick was certain. "There's more."

Sam glanced sharply to the left before he returned his gaze to Nick. "Yeah, there's more."

Nick prompted, "And?"

Sam took another sip of scotch. "Along with the files under regular encryption, which were most of them, there were some files encrypted with codes the NIH uses only for its highest security levels."

"Interesting," Nick said. *And even more disturbing*, he thought.

"Mr. H does his homework." Sam smiled without showing his teeth.

"He does." Nick clutched the flash drive in his hand, afraid to release his grip on it. He was already betting that Sidney's file was one of the ones under heavy encryption.

As Nick rushed back to his house after lunch, he surveyed the road for cops. There were none around, so he floored it.

Once back, he crashed through the door, throwing everything on the counter except for the flash drive. He headed directly to his office and shoved it into the port on his computer. As soon as everything uploaded, he started navigating through the files. Mr. H had created two folders:

one with normally encrypted data and the other with high-security encryption.

Nick scanned the first folder, and as he suspected, nothing unusual came up. He cracked his neck and moused over to the folder containing the others. The arrow hovered above the icon with cold nonchalance, unaware of what it pointed to. Seconds crawled by as Nick stared at the monitor. He closed his eyes as he thought of Melissa. Then taking a slow inhale, as if preparing for a dive into deep water, he left-clicked. Black and white organized into letters and numbers on the screen.

The files were listed alphabetically. Within a few seconds, he found Sidney's. It hadn't been lost at all, just electronically hidden. Nick opened it up. Skimming through the data, he looked for a trail.

Looked like Sidney had been at the children's home for only a few days before being given to a foster family. The listing of that relocation was the last and only one on his record. It was at least possible Sidney's foster family had adopted him, even if that hadn't been noted.

Nick drew his notepad from his chest pocket, scribbled down the address, ejected the flashdrive from the port, turned off the computer, and pushed away from his desk. He grabbed his jacket as he rushed to the garage, starting his car with his remote along the way.

CHAPTER 4

SECRETS

Melissa frowned at her phone. Nick said he hadn't taken that weird underwear case, so why wasn't he answering? Melissa typed in another message and pressed send. She shut off the screen, placing it next to her on the weight bench. Putting her gloves back on, she strode up to the punching bag, closing her eyes to regain her calm.

She pelted the bag with a hard right hook. *Whack!* Then followed the punch with several more. Sweat dripped down her forehead and into her eyes. She tried to wipe it off with the back of one of her gloves, but it just got worse.

Victoria Ilson, Melissa's sparring partner and friend, said, "Let me get you a towel, Mel."

"What? Huh?" Melissa looked over at Victoria. She was tiny, had short, spiked blond hair and striking violet eyes. Melissa had met her at this boxing gym years ago, and they had gradually become friends. Now they both worked at the same real estate agency.

Melissa looked down at the top of her glove, staring at the smear of sweat. "Yeah, sure. Thanks, Vic," she said absently. "Hold on." She took off her right glove and held it between her knees as she reached out to grab the offered towel. She mopped her forehead in a circular motion, then pulled the glove from her knees and went back to the bench. As she sank down on it, her body felt as heavy as her heart.

Melissa was troubled by what she had learned from the children's home. She loved her sweet baby boy but just wasn't ready for him when he came. She wished she had been. She hated that she'd had to give him up. But she couldn't deal with any more pain, and that was why she wouldn't let Nick find out what had happened to him. She feared the worst. Suppose it turned out that he was dead? How the hell could that help her heal?

She was afraid Nick might have lied to her about his search for Sidney. That hurt more than she cared to acknowledge. She trusted him. Or at least, she wanted to. She found it difficult to really trust anyone, growing up the way she did, but she didn't want to be that way anymore. Not trusting made her feel like she was always alone no matter who else was around.

Victoria slipped onto the bench beside her. "Something going on?" She rocked back and forth as she spoke. She never seemed to stop moving.

"Nothing a few hard punches can't solve," Melissa answered with tight diction. She was hurt, confused, and indescribably sad. But punching the bag made her feel better, sort of, so she got up to hit it some more. She fired jabs, undercuts, and hooks in quick succession, and even though each one connected with its target, she felt like she was stabbing the air. She stopped punching and stared at the bag. It was pointless.

"You do know you can talk to me, right? If you want." Victoria placed a hand on Melissa's sweaty shoulder.

Melissa gave Vic's hand a couple of pats with her boxing glove and endeavored a smile, but it didn't carry to her eyes. A tiny sigh escaped from her throat. "Yeah, I know. Thanks. I'll let you know, okay? I just need to figure this one out on my own. I appreciate the offer."

She did appreciate Vic's kindness and friendship, but she had never told her about Sidney and didn't know where to begin. Nick was the only person who knew. "Sorry, I'm not such great company."

Victoria smiled. "It's okay. Just know I'm always here for you."

CHAPTER 5

THE MYSTERIOUS UNCLE

"The destination is on your left," said the computer-generated voice of the GPS.

Nick looked over at the white, Cape Cod-style cottage. Two cars were crammed into the narrow driveway, both older models. Nick parked at the curb in front of the house and scanned the neighborhood.

What he saw was the demographic model for the typical foster care home: lower middle class, a little rundown but not outright poor. Nick knew his car looked out of place here, but he wasn't worried it was going to be stripped down and sold for parts.

He reached into his briefcase and selected one of Sam's ever-reliable government IDs. He'd acquired quite a collection. Walking to the front door of the white house, he was unusually aware of his composure, knowing if Melissa had come instead of him, she'd be frantic. He rang the doorbell three times, then knocked. Now he heard footfalls coming toward the door, followed by the sound of a deadbolt being unlocked. The door opened, and Nick found himself face-to-face with a gentle-seeming woman of middle years. She was impeccably groomed and dressed in a simple but tasteful manner. She smiled at him. "Hello."

"Hello," Nick said in a somewhat formal tone. "Are you Mrs. Jessica Walker?"

She peered at him in a mildly inquisitive way. "I am. May I ask who you are?"

"Of course. Forgive my poor manners." He extended his hand to shake hers, which she did readily. "I'm Tom Saffiano. I work with the federal oversight committee of Sunshine Children's Homes. Our team ensures that all the Sunshine Children's Homes are being run according to the high standards the President has set for them." Nick held out his badge, which Jessica looked at carefully. "I just need your help to update our records on a child that I believe you fostered several years ago. This particular child's file is only partially complete. I was hoping you could help us fill in the blanks, so to speak."

Jessica gave a quick nod. "Oh, of course. Please do come in. Can I offer you a glass of water?"

"No, I'm fine, thanks," Nick said as he stepped into the small, cozy living room, decorated in coordinating tones of ivory and soft blue-gray. It echoed refinement like the woman before him.

Jessica offered Nick a cautious smile. She appeared nervous but not overly so. "Okay, well, have a seat." She gestured toward a dove-gray sofa and sat down in an armchair.

Nick sat also and took a notebook from his briefcase. He turned it to a blank page and got a pen out of his suit jacket. He had performed this exact action more than a hundred times, in as many settings.

Jessica asked, "What child did you want to know about?"

"Sidney Ryder."

A brief look of sadness passed over Jessica's features but was quickly replaced with a benign expression. "Ah, Sidney, what about him?"

"Well, the last data entry shows that he was brought here to your home. I thought that perhaps you adopted him."

Jessica's lips tightened briefly before she answered. "Well, we certainly wanted to." Her eyes got shiny, as though she held back tears. "Sidney was such a sweet, bright baby, so incredibly inquisitive. He really was special, you know." She looked away from Nick, captured by memory. Then her eyes focused back on him. "Anyway, we were so smitten with Sidney we filed the papers to adopt him almost immediately." She sighed. "But these things tend to take time, so it wasn't until Sidney was a year old that everything was in order for us to become his mother and father legally." Jessica hesitated before she continued. "That was when his mother's uncle showed up." Every feature of her face fell at once.

Nick was positive Melissa didn't have any uncles. "The children's home has no record of any uncle."

She raised her eyebrows. "Well, as you said, that's why you're here—because Sidney's history needs to be filled in."

Nick coughed and turned his attention to his notebook. "Tell me what happened next." He held his pen high.

"Well, Henry—that's my husband—and I were devastated when we knew we were going to lose Sidney. But the man who was taking him from us was a blood relative, and the adoption hadn't been finalized yet, so there wasn't much we could do about it. He told us he loved his niece." Jessica looked down at her hands. "She had gotten into some trouble with drugs, but he had faith she would eventually get herself out of it. Her uncle was committed to taking care of Sidney for as long as it took for his niece to get herself back together."

Nick jotted in his notebook as Jessica spoke.

"Naturally," she continued, "the children's home never divulged how distraught Sidney's mother had been to give him up. It was her uncle who told us that she'd fallen in love with her son from the moment he was born and hoped to keep him, even though her pregnancy had been unwanted. But one night after a party she hosted, she was so drunk and high that she completely forgot about Sidney and left her place with her friends, leaving Sidney alone."

Nick's pen paused. Was that true? Melissa had never told him that part.

"She ended up passing out later in the evening and didn't make it back home until the next afternoon. Apparently, she was horrified when she realized she had left him alone for close to ten hours. When she returned, she knew he must be hungry and thirsty, but he could barely cry because he was so dehydrated. She realized then it wasn't fair, or safe, for her to keep him with her. So the next day she brought him to Sunshine D.C., believing they offered him his best chance to have the life he deserved."

Nick kept his body still, though his mind was agitated. He concentrated on writing very neatly.

After a moment's pause, Jessica said, "You really could see it as a blessing that Sidney's mother was aware it was the right thing."

Nick was happy he had an excuse to look down. Jessica was still talking. Nick focused on listening to her.

"So we knew it was best for Sidney to go with his uncle and eventually back to his mother, if she could change. Besides, we were so impressed that her uncle was willing to support her and to raise Sidney for as long as was necessary. Now that's a loving, supportive family. Henry and I were just surprised he didn't offer sooner. Seemed a little odd to us that he waited so long to come forward, but people have their reasons, so we didn't question it."

The lines on Jessica's face appeared to grow deeper the longer they talked. She took in a deep breath, perhaps gathering the strength to finish her story.

"It was hard to give Sidney up after having him with us for so long. But all of his great uncle's documents were in order, and he had the support of the children's home, so we packed up Sidney's things that same day. Then his great uncle took him away, and that's the last we saw of him." She stared down at her lap.

Nick wished he could say something reassuring. No words came to him. "I see," he said finally. "That is all very helpful, thank you. By the way, what did Sidney's great uncle look like?" Seeing the question on Jessica's face, he added quickly, "Just to complete the record."

Jessica's features tightened. "Yes, of course. Let's see. Hmmm, it was years ago." She looked around the room as if trying to find someone to help her. Then her countenance changed quite suddenly. "You know what, can you hold on a second? I'm going to rip my husband away from his tinkering in the basement. He'll be able to tell you. He has a much better memory than I do."

Nick had a feeling her memory was just fine, but he told her, "Okay, thanks." He leaned back into the sofa and waited for Jessica to return.

A few minutes later, she returned with a tall man of about forty-five. He had jet-black hair, and the scent of sawdust permeated the air around him. He extended a large, muscular hand toward Nick. "Hi, I'm Henry. My wife said you wanted me to describe Sidney's great uncle to you."

Nick nodded. "Yes, if you can. Whatever you can remember would be very helpful."

"Oh, I can. No problem. That man made an impression on me. He wasn't the type of guy I would have pictured being related to Sidney. For one thing, he was pretty damn short, and we knew Sidney was in one of the highest percentiles for height for his age." Henry Walker rubbed his chin as he looked up and to the right, trying to reconstruct an image in his mind. "I would say he was about five-feet-six-inches tall. He was pudgy, completely bald, and wore small, round wire-rimmed eyeglasses. Sidney was only a baby at the time, but it was obvious he was going to grow up to be a hell of a lot more handsome than that guy."

Jessica's cheeks turned red. "Henry!" she scolded. But Nick thought she agreed with her husband's assessment.

Nick asked, "Do you remember what color his eyes were?"

"No, but I think they were dark, and they were definitely small, and so was his mouth. And his feet—that man had incredibly small feet. Oh yeah, one more thing: his shoes were so shiny. Goddamn, were they shiny! It looked like he'd had them lacquered. I've never seen such shiny shoes."

Nick made some quick notes. He looked back up at Henry. "And about how old would you say he was?"

"I'd guess about forty-five or fifty. But hard to tell because he was bald, you know? Sometimes that makes a man look older than he is."

"True," Nick commented. "Any other details you can remember?"

Henry thought for a minute and shook his head. "No, that's it."

Nick reached into the pocket of his suit jacket and retrieved a business card. "Okay, well, I guess that's all, then. Thank you, both for your time." He handed the card to Henry. "My number's on the back of the card. If either of you thinks of anything else, just call me."

CHAPTER 6

THE CENTER FOR INTERACTIVE RESEARCH AND SOLUTIONS

The Center for Interactive Research and Applied Solutions, or CIRAS, shone in the sunlight so intensely it almost blinded Dr. Jack Kerwin. He brought a hand to his brow to block the glare. His pale blue eyes traced the places where expanses of glass and metal entwined. The design was both formidable and seductive. He took in a deep breath to balance his nerves.

Jack pushed his fingers through his sandy-blond hair—a nervous habit—as he walked in a semi-trance state toward CIRAS's façade. He stopped in front of its huge glass doors and frowned. As far as he could tell, there was no obvious way to enter. Standing motionless, he contemplated his options. Before he had time to decide what to do next, blue lasers emitted from two smooth, triangular posts flanking the entrance. The beams passed over Jack's athletic six-foot-three body. He had the uneasy feeling he was being scanned from the inside out.

Snorting, Jack realized he was probably right. He'd be sure to encounter lots of high-tech security during his stay at CIRAS. It was the most technologically advanced research facility in the world. Still, he didn't like being scrutinized.

The gargantuan doors glided open, and Jack stepped into CIRAS's vast foyer. *Well,* he said to himself with his typical good humor, *guess they realize I'm me.*

The cavernous internal space, also composed of glass and metal, was a less shiny echo of its exterior. The combination of materials made it seem as if a subtle light emanated from all exposed surfaces in a creepy-cool sort of way. The floor was fabricated from a material similar to solid quartz but more exotic looking. It was beautiful but cold. Jack wasn't sure he liked it, but he found himself intrigued.

Despite his scientific interest, Jack didn't want to be left alone here with his unnerving sci-fi influenced thoughts. He stood tall, trying not to squirm, the lines on his brow turning into crevasses as he looked around. Running his hand through his hair again, he wondered where everyone was. Maybe he should try to call the director of the facility, Dr. Scott Maxwell, and find out where he should go?

In almost direct response to his thoughts, a panel slid open in the seemingly solid wall to his right. His eyes widened. Like it was a scene straight out of Hollywood, a stunningly beautiful woman walked toward him. She wore a three-quarter-sleeve, ivory sheath dress that blended seamlessly with the creamy skin of her slim neck, arms, and legs. The monotone palette was a pleasing contrast to her lustrous red hair and green eyes. She was about five foot eight, but her heels were so high that she stood only a few inches shorter than Jack. An inevitable frisson of sexual attraction played down his body, which he tried hard to ignore in the interest of professionalism.

The woman spoke. Though Jack tried to focus on her words instead of her appearance, it was nearly impossible. She was the finest-looking woman he had ever seen. Virtually perfect. He swallowed and smiled, hoping he didn't look like a love-struck or even worse—horny teenager.

"Dr. Kerwin, welcome." She reached a hand out and shook Jack's. "Ellen Standis. So pleased to meet you. Was your trip here okay?"

Jack nodded. He was afraid that if he spoke, something inappropriate might come out of his mouth. He didn't have much practice dealing with this sort of distraction at work. And considering how much he had to focus on his work, that was a good thing.

"Excellent." Her full lips curved into a sexy smile.

Jack drew in a breath and blinked away his improper thought.

"Your bags have already arrived and been brought to your rooms. Later today there will be a residents' meeting you'll need to attend. For now, I'll show you to your apartment so you can get settled in."

"Sounds perfect!" His tone was excited and a little too high, so he deepened it when he added, "Lead the way."

"What's your area of research?" Ellen asked as they walked through the twisting corridors.

"I'm looking for a genetic cure to childhood leukemia."

"A noble cause. Are you close?"

"I hope so. I feel like I've been just one puzzle piece away from the whole thing slipping into place for a few years. Who knows? I may never get there."

"Your Tabula Rasa group will help you," she said matter-of-factly. "They help everyone."

"That would be great. It's why I'm here."

"They will."

She stopped in front of a door on their right. "We're here." She pointed at a flat electronic pad in the wall. "Just wave your hand over that, and the door will open."

Jack tried it and heard the door click. "Cool." He grinned at her like a little boy then thought maybe he shouldn't have been so excited by it. Still, it definitely *was* cool. Besides, he wouldn't be able to hide the fact that he was a nerd for very long.

Ellen giggled. "Yeah, it is kind of fun, isn't it?"

The way she laughed was sexy, too. *Focus, Jack. Focus.* He placed a hand on the door and pushed it open, angling his head back towards her. "See you at the meeting tonight?"

She nodded. "I'll be there."

Jack arrived at the conference room just before it started and slipped into a chair next to Ellen. At the front of the room, two men he recognized only from pictures, Dr. Scott Maxwell and Dr. Randolph Jameson, stood next to one another. Maxwell drew his eyebrows together and frowned at Jack as he got situated next to Ellen.

Jameson was the founding father of CIRAS, and Maxwell, who had once been Jameson's young protégé, now ran it as the director. To Jack, they looked like Dr. Jekyll and Mr. Hyde. Jameson was well built and handsome, with a kind air about him. Maxwell was short and bald, with a protruding belly, and, based on the earlier and still persisting frown, a disagreeable demeanor.

Jameson spoke first, gazing warmly at the assembled group. "Welcome to CIRAS. You each hold the honor of being one of the four residents we accept yearly. I don't need to tell you what the competition is like to attain that honor. You all already know."

There were murmurs of agreement and nervous laughs from the group.

Jameson continued. "CIRAS has been directly responsible for many scientific achievements, including the creation of bio-renewable fuel, weather control that combats global warming, low-cost desalination plants, and even the cure for male-pattern baldness."

Jack chuckled, along with another man nearby who had a full head of dark hair.

Maxwell spoke. "You will each be assigned to a Tabula Rasa group. These are exceptionally intelligent, highly trained individuals. We expect you to take full advantage of their intellects. CIRAS does not tolerate failure." Maxwell glared at them and placed his clasped hands on his round stomach as though resting them on a shelf. He sighed as though they were all a bother to him and he would rather be someplace else.

Jameson threw Maxwell a sideways glance that seemed to express displeasure. "What Dr. Maxwell means is that we are very confident you will get the answers you are looking for. We are available to each of you if you need us."

Maxwell confirmed this statement with a smile that looked pasted on his face. Jack knew whom he'd be going to for help if he needed it.

Jameson concluded. "Now we're going to leave you with Ms. Standis, whom you all have been introduced to already. She'll help you get acquainted with each other."

Jack found himself following Jameson and Maxwell as they headed to the exit. It looked like Maxwell was grumbling under his breath, chastising Jameson for something.

Behind him, Ellen asked, "Jack, will you join us?"

Jack turned. Ellen and the other residents were gathering around a conference table in the back of the room. "Yeah, sorry." He quickly took a seat.

Ellen spoke to the three men and solitary woman seated at the large, sleek table. "I think the easiest way to begin is to go around the table and tell us all your name and what project you will work on while you're here. You don't need to share the details of your work. Just the general focus will be adequate." She smiled at Jack as she nodded his way. "You first, Dr. Kerwin."

"Hi, everyone. I'm Jack Kerwin, and I'm here researching a genetically-based cure for childhood leukemia."

"Okay, great," said Ellen. "Let's continue clockwise, shall we?"

A petite Asian American woman spoke next. "I'm Rachel Woo. I'm working on creating airborne vaccines for use in developing countries."

The next resident said, "Yes, um, I'm Elvis Vitali. I'm developing a brain chip for language learning."

The last member spoke. "And I would be Prashant Chaudri. I work in the field of cybernetic brains."

Chaudri's speech sounded computer-generated, and it made Jack smile. He had gotten used to the fact that many scientists had socially stiff personalities, but it still amused him at times.

He returned his focus to Ms. Standis. Nothing stiff about her. She was all soft curves and feminine and... He swallowed hard and concentrated on what she was saying, trying to use her voice as a rappel line toward more reasoned thinking.

"You make quite an impressive group." The group tittered with nervous laughter. Ellen cleared her throat and continued in a more serious tone. "But be aware all research conducted here will remain in house until you get permission from Dr. Maxwell to share any findings. To be clear, you're not permitted even a phone call or email to a colleague outside of CIRAS."

Optimism left the room as though someone shut the light off. Researchers were used to bouncing ideas and opinions off mentors, colleagues, anyone who could help answer a question that needed answering. Everyone sat very still. Jack saw Dr. Vitali gulp.

Seeming to sense the change in atmosphere, Ellen pulled herself taller. "You are, however, free to speak with one another. A list with all your contact information will be sent to each of you."

Dr. Woo frowned.

Ellen continued. "I'll send you an electronic manual outlining the guidelines more explicitly. Make sure you sign the agreement or you'll be denied access to your group."

Jack had a life-long habit of avoiding signing anything he didn't absolutely have to. He walked away from the evening's meeting with apprehension and curiosity circling through him like two opposing forces, wondering what exactly, he'd gotten himself into.

CHAPTER 7

INVISIBLE THINK TANK

J ack entered his apartment, which resembled a suite in a five-star hotel, or at least what they looked like in movies. Truth was it was better appointed than any hotel he'd ever stayed in. Why had they gone to all this trouble? The opportunity of a lifetime had nothing to do with thread-count.

One room seemed particularly out of place. The strange compartment was portioned off with thick glass walls rising to the ceiling, parted only by a narrow gap to facilitate entry. Jack's shoulders were broad, and as he sidestepped through the entry, claustrophobia threatened. The translucence of the cell-like room fell into the CIRAS category of creepy-cool. Would he feel like a monitored lab rat, working within its confines? His jaw clenched against the notion.

Looking around the cell, he saw an L-shaped table bearing two identical tabletop workstations occupying most of the space. Each included a micro-thin computer monitor secured to a console and a permanently fixed tablet with an electronic pen. Jack searched for a power button on both but couldn't find one.

He plunked himself down in front of the left-side console to continue his search. As soon as his rear contacted the chair, the computer powered up.

A disembodied voice welcomed him. "Good Evening, Dr. Kerwin. May I call you Jack?"

"Huh?" Jack startled then figured it out. "Sure. What the hell should I call you?"

"Whatever you wish."

Jack considered briefly then said in a British accent, "How about I call you Computer?" Just like Captain Picard from the Starship Enterprise. He smiled to himself. It was childish and more than a little nerdy, but he couldn't help himself.

"That will do," the voice responded without humor. "I see that you have received a communication. Would you like me to read the document out loud, or shall I simply display it on the screen?"

Jack sat back in his chair and crossed his arms. "Um, how about both?"

"Of course."

Jack listened to the electronic voice and glanced up periodically at the displayed text. Not much of the information was new to him. CIRAS had been quite clear that there would be many guidelines—i.e., restrictions—which he would have to follow if he was accepted into its program. He hadn't hesitated to agree, as the opportunity far outweighed the inconvenience created by the neurotic possessiveness of the center. Jack was barely paying attention when something the computer said jarred him out of his boredom. He focused on the screen, brows knitted, and read:

Protocol Regarding Interaction With Tabula Rasa

"Can you repeat what you just said?"

"The Tabula Rasa component you will be paired with will have all its work displayed on the computer and tablet to your right. There will be a continual flow of their findings and recommendations on that computer. But you can always scroll up or down to access any part of the TR data."

"Okay." That seemed pretty straightforward. "When is our first meeting?"

"There will be no meetings."

"What?"

"Tabula Rasa members prefer digital-only interaction, but what they lack in social skills is offset by their prowess with problem solving."

"What the hell! Sometimes I'm going to need to talk face-to-face. There are times it's the only way to hash through problems."

"That's not possible."

"Why not?"

"As I've stated, they prefer digital interaction—"

He heard the tightness in his voice. "I've never done research where you can't actually talk to other human beings."

"There's a first time for everything."

"Screw you," Jack screamed, instantly feeling ridiculous. *Computer*, was a computer, after all. "Sorry, goodnight." *Equally stupid.*

"Goodnight, Dr. Kerwin."

Jack brought up the document and fixed his vision on the monitor. He was paying attention now, his interest piqued by suspicion and anger.

```
Should you choose not to abide by these
guidelines and make public, in any manner,
this private knowledge, CIRAS retains the
means to prevent your involvement in further
research within the United States and with
prominent partner facilities internationally.
```

Jack reread the last statement to make sure he had it right. They threatened to blackball him. He continued reading.

```
Should you sign the agreement and later
violate its terms, CIRAS will reclaim its
ownership of all scholarship conducted at its
facility and repossess all subsequent research
based on Tabula Rasa findings. CIRAS will
employ any means necessary to do so.
```

Betray us and you will die a slow, painful academic death. And oh, by the way, you will never work again. Great. He read more, but it was just more inventive ways of saying the same thing. And something about every session in the "office" being recorded

His body vibrated with resentment as he examined every inch of the space, looking for any type of recording device. He found nothing. *Did you think they would be out here in the open for you to find? This is so messed up...*

Jack stopped as he realized that according to this damn agreement even his auto-conversation would be recorded. He felt tricked—used.

He hadn't felt that way since a professor in one of his graduate courses had claimed Jack's work as his own. He had already accepted that he would be observed while he was at CIRAS, but he now had to consider that he might have no privacy at all for a year.

Jack closed his eyes and took long, slow breaths, using a technique his sensei had taught him. New, unwelcome thoughts piggybacked his exhalations and powered their way into his consciousness. Do you actually care what you have to go through to find this cure? What about the other children who have the same disease that Jeremy died from? You might be able to save them and their families from so much pain.

He would sign the agreement.

Paranoid or not, Scott Maxwell ran the best research facility in the world. Nobody would pass up the chance to come here. And nobody did. If some previous invitee had already revealed CIRAS's dark side—whatever it was—the entire academic community would know in the time it took a particle of light to circle the Earth.

Jack took in yet another deep breath and allowed his burgeoning resentment to deflate. If Maxwell wanted to play his little control games, Jack would try to pretend he wasn't bothered by it.

It wasn't like anyone was getting hurt.

CHAPTER 8

A HELLUVA LOT OF UNCLES

Nick flung the last file onto the rising manila mountain. He stared at the tottering pile and thought of Melissa. She had a habit of making fun of him for printing everything out. He admitted the practice dated him, but he didn't really care. It still made more sense to him to hold paper in his hands. Besides, he liked it when Melissa teased him.

Somewhere in there was the NIH's secret. Nick flipped meticulously through each page in every folder. All the encrypted records concluded just like Sidney's had. The documented child was given to a foster home, and then the file ended abruptly.

Nick compared these high-security files to some of the normal ones that were part of a control group. In these, a child's history was always followed either to the point of adoption or adulthood. There were no exceptions, and that meant something. Some of these foster families must still be living in the D.C. area. He took out a red pen and started to circle addresses. He compiled his list, got dressed appropriately, and headed out the door.

Nick was almost done with his interview of Mr. Frank Sosa, who sat opposite him at Sosa's kitchen table. The man made a single, conglomerate fist with both his hands and rested it on the table's edge. He lifted his gaze to Nick. "So that was the end of that."

"Let me guess what her great uncle looked like."

Frank regarded Nick with a strange look. "Huh?"

Nick realized his mistake immediately. "Sorry. I got confused for a minute. I've talked to so many families today, my head is spinning." He smiled apologetically. "Why don't you describe him to me?"

Nick didn't need to listen to Frank's answer.

Five minutes later, he wrenched open the back door of his car and stuffed the file into the tote on his back seat. He ripped off his suit jacket and hurled it on top. Melissa liked him to hang his suit jackets up so they wouldn't get wrinkled, but right now he couldn't be bothered. He slammed the back door and thrust his body into the front seat. The tires of his black Audi screeched as he peeled away from the curb. The veins in his hands bulged as he gripped the steering wheel. "Every single one of them has the same damned uncle. That's a damn lot of sisters!"

Seven foster families and not one of them had successfully adopted any of the Sunshine children, though three of them had hoped to. Their stories ended the same. Some supposed uncle came to the foster home to take the child. They all described him with the same characteristics that Henry Walker attributed to Sidney's great-uncle.

Nick drove onto the interstate. "Call Sam Prezziato," he told his car's computer.

"Hey," Sam answered. "What do you need? I only have a few minutes."

"Have you ever heard any weird rumors circling around Sunshine Children's Homes? Missing kids, hidden records, stuff like that?"

"No, can't say that I have. Aren't they supposed to be some sort of super-duper orphanage?" Sam laughed as if making a joke, which it wasn't.

Nick didn't laugh back. "Yeah, they are. But it's starting to look like they might be hiding something. Something big. Can you ask around for me, see if anyone knows anything?"

"Yeah, sure. You know the rate."

"What? No price increase?"

"Don't test me," Sam said with a laugh in his voice.

Nick had caught him at a good time. "I should know better after all these years."

"Yeah, you should."

Nick smiled. He segued into the other reason for his call. "Oh, and could you search government databases for a suspect's description, see if there's a match? It's for a different case."

"Yeah, okay. Just text me the details and give me a few days. I need to get off the phone now."

"Thanks, Sam."

"You're welcome." Sam actually sounded like he meant it, exposing a sliver of the true persona beneath his vigilantly constructed exterior.

CHAPTER 9

MENACING MAFIA

Nick rolled his eyes the moment he saw Sam's ultra-stretch limo, a glaring contrast to the other vehicles in this public parking lot. Sam cherished his limousines and all the other tangible indicators of his success and liked to flaunt them.

He extended a hand toward the door of the limo. It opened with a click just before his fingers could reach the handle. Inside, Sam moved away from the door to let Nick in. Sam wore Armani again and held the expected glass of scotch in his left hand.

Nick closed the door behind him and took a seat along the right side. "Looking impeccable as always."

"I try, Nick. A man has to try." Sam cleared his throat and took a lazy sip of scotch. He gestured to his glass. "Want some?"

"Yeah, what the hell." Sam started to get up, but Nick stopped him. "I got it." He slid along the leather seat and poured a glass for himself from the bar.

Nick lifted his glass. "Salud."

Sam echoed, "Salud." They each took a sip of the expensive scotch.

Nick got right to it. "You have the information?"

"Yes and no."

"You know I hate that kind of answer." He looked Sam in the eyes. "You hate that kind of answer, too. What's going on?"

Prezziato shrugged. Nick wasn't sure if it was a smug gesture or a guilty one. "Yeah, well, you happen to be asking some very tricky questions. But, first things first. Nothing yet on that guy you asked me to look into. I haven't been able to access the ... uh ... right data banks yet." They both knew Sam meant his inside government guys hadn't been able to illegally tap into them. The two of them were in the habit of politely ignoring these types of uncomfortable facts, given that Nick's past employer happened to be the US government.

Sam twisted his lips and sniffed at the same time, looking discomfited. "The Sunshine Children's Home stuff, that's a little different."

"But, you have information?"

"Like I said, yes and no." Prezziato tilted his glass back and forth to emphasize each word. "I know you don't want to hear it, but it happens to be the truth."

"Okay, okay, I take your word for it. Just tell me what that means."

Sam nodded slowly. "It's good that you're bowing to my superior intelligence."

Nick gave him a false smile and downed the rest of his scotch.

"Let me give you a little background," Sam began. "You know that I run a respectable business, Nick."

Nick fought the impulse to roll his eyes again. It wouldn't be wise to do that at this juncture.

"But the nature of my business requires that I keep in contact with some less reputable organizations. In particular, I have certain dealings with a larger group which polices many city goings-on." He flourished his right hand in a general exterior direction.

"You mean the Mafia?" Despite the widespread belief that D.C. didn't have any organized crime lords, he and Prezziato—and the US government, quite frankly—knew that wasn't true. The FBI monitored a secret underground network that, while small, had been entrenched in the city for decades. The government tolerated their existence so they could exploit the network's connections.

"That's what some call them. I prefer not to use that word."

"But that is the organization you're speaking of?"

"Well, yes. Yes, it is." He nodded. "Now what was I saying? Hmmm, would you pour me a drink while I try to remember?"

Nick ignored his petulance, refilling his glass with more scotch and handing it to him.

Prezziato took an extraordinarily slow sip. "Ah, it seems to have come back to me. As I was saying, I have a certain amount of contact with these organizations. And when I inquired about Sunshine Children's Homes, it was suggested to me that it would perhaps be best not to ask any more questions. To let the matter drop, as it were."

"They threatened you?"

Sam shook his head. Nick still sensed an undertone of guilt in him. "I wouldn't say they went as far as that. They were just making a strong recommendation. I suggest you follow it."

"Can't do that, Sam."

He shrugged. "All right. Your call." He drank the rest of his scotch. When he leveled his eyes at Nick, they belied his nonchalant attitude. "Don't say you haven't been warned."

"So, what? You won't help me?"

"I will help in the matter of trying to find the described gentleman, as long as he has no association with Sunshine Children's Homes."

Nick hated it when Sam talked in that overly formal fashion, like he was some kind of English lord instead of an Italian-born punk, but when Sam started talking that way, it also meant he felt threatened and that was important to note. "Okay, thanks. And thanks for the scotch. Let me know what you find out." He exited the limousine and stepped out into the daylight, which suddenly seemed too bright.

CHAPTER 10

THE PROBLEM WITH EINSTEIN

J ack paced in his suite, asking himself what else he would have to sacrifice, besides his sense of privacy and self-respect. Possibilities tumbled around noisily in his head like rocks in a polisher.

Eventually, his capacity to control his mind triumphed. There was just one good reason to persevere here at CIRAS, and he let it sustain him like an air tank sustains a diver. If he could keep other kids from having to go through what his brother Jeremy had experienced, nothing else mattered. Not really. What was personal privacy when compared with saving children from pain or death? Jack would have given anything to keep Jeremy alive. He would have made a pact with the devil. *I might be getting ready to do just that.*

Jack sunk into the chair in his office. The gleaming walls felt like they might fall down and crush him. With a determined blink and a soul-deep sigh, he opened his mouth to speak the fateful words, the words that would sign away his freedom. He held his mouth open, procrastinating. His tongue could dry out before he capitulated. *No, I will do this thing,* he thought. Then—*It better be damned worth it.*

"Computer."

Screens blinked on. "Yes, Jack."

"I want to sign the agreement. Get it up for me."

"Of course." The page appeared instantly.

Seeing it froze him up. His jaw felt locked.

"Jack?" the computer inquired.

His shoulders shuddered. "How do I do it?"

"Just sign with the pen on the tablet."

Jack looked down and picked up the electronic pen. He held it above the signature line, where it wavered, just like his will. *Jeremy,* his conscience reminded him. He brought the pen down and signed his name, *Dr. Jack Kerwin.* It was done. Now he could get to work.

Except some force within him objected. He found himself heading to the gym, where he commenced a very sweaty two-hour workout. After that, he caught up on the latest news from CNN and Fox. Then he indulged in a one-and-a-half-hour-long lunch at one of CIRAS's restaurants. Post-lunch, he took a long walk through the manicured grounds and returned inside for a visit to the in-house bar.

Each step he took toward the bar summoned an admonishment. He should be working. He had no business drinking and relaxing. Had he forgotten about Jeremy?

Jack answered the voice: Yes, he should be working. No, he shouldn't be drinking. He hadn't forgotten Jeremy. But he did need some time to recover. The way he felt was similar to what it was like when he lost a soccer match. It took time to recoup before he could start concentrating on his next game.

He turned the next corner and ran into Ellen Standis. Literally. He had been looking down at his shoes and didn't see her.

"Hey," he said. She looked hot. There was no other way to put it. She wore snug jeans and a silky black top, and he thought she looked even better than she had in that sexy white dress.

Ellen slipped a hand into her right pocket and tilted her head to the side. "Hi, Jack. I was looking for you, but you weren't in your room."

Jack looked around the hallway like she might be talking to a different Jack. "Who, me?"

She threw her head back and laughed. "Yeah, you."

He ran a hand through his hair. "Well, here I am."

"Yes, here you are. I wanted you to take me for a drink."

Jack was confused. He liked Ellen, and he liked sex. He really liked sex. But he never mixed sex with work. Not to say that was what she was offering. But his work at CIRAS was very important. He couldn't afford to screw things up or to get distracted. Besides, why was she interested in him when she could have anyone she wanted?

Drawing strongly upon his self-discipline, he said, "Sorry, Ellen, I'm busy. Maybe another time." He held his breath.

"Oh, that's a pity."

Jack pushed his hands into his pockets. He didn't meet her eyes. "Another time, I promise."

She regarded him for a long moment, as if she were solving a complex math problem in her head. "Okay, Jack. But next time I won't accept any excuses." She turned to go back the way she'd come. Jack couldn't resist watching her backside as she left. He sighed.

He opened the door to the small bar on the top floor of CIRAS. His eyes widened when he saw Dr. Elvis Vitali seated on a futuristic metallic cylinder—CIRAS's version of a barstool. Jack tapped him on the shoulder. Dr. Vitali turned around and smiled warmly. "Dr. Kerwin."

Jack found a hint of a smile. "Call me Jack."

"Sure, Jack. Call me Elvis, okay? Join me for a drink?" Elvis motioned to the seat beside him.

Jack remained standing with one hand steadied on the bar. "Yeah, that sounds good."

"What'll you have?"

Jack didn't answer the question right away. He peered around, distracted by the ultra-modern shapes and materials dispersed throughout the room. The heavy-handed décor felt forced and antagonistic, as if representative of other things that were dark, cold, and unfeeling. "Everything around here is so space-age." Jack gestured to the odd triangular glass that Elvis held.

"Yeah, sort of cool but creepy at the same time."

Jack snorted. "Exactly."

He sat down on the metallic cylinder next to Elvis and squirmed uneasily as he tried to adjust to its unusual smoothness. "I would love to sit on a good, old-fashioned bar stool right about now." He remembered he'd never answered Elvis. "I'll have whatever you're having."

"Gin and tonic with a twist," Elvis ordered from the young, skinny man behind the bar. He was dressed in black.

Jack joked, "Seems crazy they have an actual human bartender here. I would expect a robot or a synthesizer."

"Yeah, you would think that, compared with the rest of the crazy shit they've done here, creating androids—or at least highly functional robots—would be a piece of cake." Elvis looked down at the bar. "And you know what? How many people even use this bar? They probably could have made it self-serve in some funky way. Like you said, a synthesizer."

"Bet this guy's here to spy on us." Jack jerked his head toward the bartender, even though the man stared right at him. Jack didn't care. This place was screwed up, and his patience was wearing thin.

Elvis wrinkled his nose, frowning.

"Guess that wasn't funny. Too close to the truth."

"Yup." Elvis was a nerd, but he didn't seem naive. He and Jack were the same in that respect. Elvis took a deep swallow from his glass and placed it back down on the bar carefully—too carefully. How much had he drunk before Jack arrived?

The young bartender set Jack's drink in front of him, seemingly unconcerned with their conversation. The glass created a peculiar reflection on the strange surface. It was disorienting, like being on acid. Jack tried to blink away the image.

Jack gave the skinny man a quick nod. "Thanks."

The bartender nodded and walked toward the far end of the bar. He turned his back to them and occupied himself with the computer monitor located there.

As Jack picked up his glass the triangular shape pressed against his hand, making it awkward to grip. He lifted it in Elvis's direction. "To successful research."

"Successful research." Elvis's tone was flat. He looked like he wanted to say something but held back. Finally, he said, "It's weird how they do it, isn't it?"

"How who does what?" Jack slanted his eyes toward the bartender, but he was far away, and his back was still turned away from them.

"How TR does your research for you, like they don't even need you at all. You know, they display all their work on those damned computers and tablets while you sit back and twiddle your thumbs. It isn't much of a collaboration, if you ask me."

Jack didn't comment, so Elvis went on.

"I mean, they're coming up with some pretty awesome shit." Elvis heaved out a breath. "It's quite brilliant. I wish it didn't feel so weird." Elvis slugged down a large portion of his cocktail in one gulp as he squirmed around on his stool. "I hate to admit it but I don't feel like the work is mine. They're looking at the problem in a way I would've never considered. Too damn blinded by my own beliefs, I guess." He took another chug from his gin and tonic. "That's what they said they would do, but ... I'm rambling. How's your research going?"

Jack pressed his lips together and peered down at his drink. "I, um, haven't started yet." He poured the rest of his drink down his throat and slammed the empty glass on the bar.

"Why not?"

"I don't think my self-esteem has quite recovered. That agreement was quite a doozy."

Elvis coughed. "Yeah, well. I don't think your ego is going to like how it feels when you do start working with your TR group, if your research goes anything like mine has. They don't need us, so why do they want us? Why bother? Seems to me like that godforsaken think tank could solve all the world's problems if they wanted to. It's pretty emasculating." He leaned back as much as the strange stool would allow, crossing his arms over his chest.

"Tabula Rasa isn't trained to think about the problems we bring, just the solutions. They need us to give them problems so they can have something to which they can apply their intellect."

Elvis glanced at him peripherally. "You're not making me feel any better, Jack."

Jack frowned. Elvis should have known all this already. "No, but you know of Dr. Jameson's research, right? The work that was the basis for CIRAS?"

"Yeah." Elvis sounded uninterested. "Train the mind to be free of professional prejudice by rigorously avoiding the work of previous researchers. Then use the mind like a human computer—completely unbiased, but with all the beautiful ability that is unique to humankind. Then you can make that quantum leap in thought that computers can't manage. Honestly, it's all blah, blah, blah to me. Don't be offended, Jack, but I don't particularly care about the theory CIRAS was based on." Elvis stared at the bottles lined up against the back of the bar. "Even if it does mess with me now and again."

"It's worth understanding."

Elvis smiled indulgently. His eyes weren't quite in focus. "Go 'head," he slurred.

"Seems to me that if you really wanted to keep your mind blank, it would be intensely difficult to ever do any research yourself, because you would become too influenced by it. Jameson always used the example of Einstein. After Einstein developed his special and general theories of relativity, he was never truly creative again. He just kept trying to jam the discoveries of others down the throat of the special and general theories. And like stubborn children told they should 'take their medicine,' they wouldn't swallow. Remember the whole EPR fiasco with his mysterious hidden variables?"

Elvis nodded woozily.

"Who knows what Einstein would have discovered if he could've continued to look at things with the unprejudiced imagination of his youth?" Jack inhaled an impassioned breath. "If Einstein could have persisted in the mindset that nature gave him, he could have helped discover so much more." Jack was getting worked up, and he felt annoyed with Elvis's ignorance. "Were you aware that the members of Tabula Rasa are trained in all methods of mathematics, deductive reasoning, and probably other things we don't even know about? They have methods of analysis that are unique to CIRAS and highly advanced."

Elvis arched his eyebrows. "You seem pretty excited for someone who hasn't even accessed TR yet." He turned away and cleared his throat to get the attention of the bartender. "I'll have another."

"Me, too," Jack said. How many drinks would he need to get through this year? That was an algorithm he didn't want to construct. He looked back at Elvis. "Yeah, well, my feelings on the subject of TR and CIRAS are mixed, to say the least."

"That, my friend, I completely understand." Elvis made a toast in Jack's general direction.

They stayed at the bar for hours. Their conversation dwindled, and after a certain point, the only words they used were "one" and "more."

CHAPTER 11

DESIRE MEETS DECEPTION

J ack scarcely made it back to his apartment. The corridors were difficult enough to navigate sober, now it was nearly impossible. His journey became a series of challenging decisions, and he made several wrong turns. When he got to his door, he fired a fist pump as if he scored a goal.

He held his hand over the entry pad, then he was in. *Home?* Upon seeing the glass cell in the room's center, Jack sobered. Slightly. This door, this room, this goddamned facility was the reason he was drunk in the first place. CIRAS's demands ripped him down the center, making him choose between his principles and achieving his life's dream.

Time to suck it up and begin what he was here to do. Damn that he was drunk. Damn that he didn't quite know where to begin. Damn that thoughts of Ellen dropped back into his mind. Damn. Damn. Damn it all.

Jack walked into the translucent chamber. This time he wasn't walking out until he turned TR on. "Computer!" He slid into the chair.

"Yes, Jack."

"Bring Tabula Rasa online."

"Changed your mind, Jack?"

"Screw you!" He slapped his palm on the desk.

Hearing a sound, Jack cocked his head. He couldn't figure out what it was at first then he pieced it together. *Someone's knocking, idiot. Go see who it is.*

Ellen stood in the hallway. Her silky top hugged her curves, and her tight jeans showed off her perfect legs. And those heels...damn! He tried to force the thoughts that arose out of his brain. It wasn't easy. And, it wasn't working. He raked a hand through his hair, trying to get a grip on himself.

"Hey Jack, you made me a promise. I intend for you to keep it." Ellen placed her hands on her hips in a way that made an arrow.

Jesus. What promise? The one to have drinks later? She didn't look like she was here for drinks but what the hell did he know? He was drunk, and Ellen was the hottest woman he'd ever seen. His body nearly shook as he tried to resist the magnetic pull he felt towards her. It was a classic story—nerdy scientist attracted to a gorgeous secretary. He gulped as he stared, fearing he might have drowned his self-discipline in all those gin-and-tonics.

Should he try to kiss her? He wanted that and more—much, much more, but he didn't want to screw it up and lose his opportunity. *Was* there an opportunity?

Ellen shifted one clearly delineated hip to the side. "You could ask me in."

"Oh, of course, come in." Jack stepped back and held the door open. Ellen slipped inside and brushed against him. "Um, can I offer you a drink?"

"No, thank you."

"Can I get you anything? Do you want to sit down?"

She drew close to him, pushing against the tightened muscles of his abs and thighs. "That's not why I came, Jack."

He widened his eyes, pulling in a short breath. Straightening to his full height, he drew his shoulders back so the fabric of his t-shirt stretched across his pecs. He might be a nerd but he also was an accomplished soccer player and his body showed it. He never had any trouble "getting" girls, but his intrinsic southern good manners always fought with his natural sensuality. Nevertheless. "Why did you come, Ellen?"

Ellen glanced at his chest muscles then looked into his eyes. "To see you."

"Obviously. Why?"

"If you can't tell, you're not as smart as you're supposed to be." She moved closer until she was only inches away from him and leaned forward, offering her lips to his. Alcohol still clouded his judgment, but he was too carnally focused to care. Jack moved toward her, his need primal. She had come to him at just the right moment, and he would make sure she didn't regret it. He kissed her deep and hard, gripping the nape of her neck in both hands, letting his nails bite into her just a bit.

Ellen pulled away. "Thought you'd be like this."

His breath was ragged. "What?"

She stepped closer so that her breasts pushed into his chest. "Sexy, strong... sensual."

He gave her a dark smile, placing his hands on her shoulders and pulling her body into a tight line with his, his arousal obvious.

She grabbed him over his lightweight khaki pants, a glint of playfulness in her green eyes.

Jack hoped Ellen wasn't a tease or a disappointment. Gorgeous women often were.

She unzipped his pants. *Jesus!* He bit his lip.

It was more than tempting to let Ellen go on, but Jack was smarter than that. He didn't want to have sex with her just this once. He wanted to have sex with her every single day and night as long as his yearlong research grant lasted. He didn't have a genius IQ for nothing. He slipped his hands underneath her armpits and lifted her up with intentional gentleness. "Your turn."

"I'm not done."

"Don't worry, there will be more of that."

She started to pull up her top.

"My job."

Scott Maxwell settled back in his seat, his face lit by the ambient light from the monitors. The surveillance room was his favorite in all of CIRAS, other than the rooms that made up the TR Center. Four large screens nestled among a network of many smaller screens. In the center of this arrangement was the largest screen of all, showing any visual feed sent to it.

Maxwell picked up the remote control he'd designed and changed the image displayed on the largest screen. It displayed Elvis Vitali staring at his computer. His eyes gleamed, looking like he was on drugs. Perfect.

Next, he flipped over to Prashant Chaudri's apartment. The image looked the same, except that Chaudri was Indian rather than Italian. Maxwell was pleased. He pressed the remote again—Woo, same as the others. The corners of his mouth turned up. They were all exactly where he expected them to be.

He pressed a few buttons. Now, the larger screen showed the live images from Jack Kerwin's office. Kerwin wasn't at his computer. Maxwell put the remote down and operated one of the video game-like controls to the right of his reclining chair. He toggled around until the scene on the large monitor displayed a wider view of Kerwin's apartment.

Just to the left of his apartment door, Ellen crouched down in front of the researcher. The corners of Maxwell's mouth reached up higher as he watched her distract him from all his fuss about signing the agreement. She was doing an admirable job. Maxwell liked it when all was right in the world. It was hard work keeping the idiots in line.

"Jesus Christ, Scott!"

Maxwell startled, turning to see Randolph Jameson.

"Shut that thing off!" Jameson spat. "Have you no decency?"

Maxwell gave him a lazy glance. "You could have knocked."

Jameson gritted his teeth. "I did knock."

Maxwell shrugged. "Guess I didn't hear you. What do you want?"

"Turn these things off first. You know how I feel about them."

Maxwell sneered. "And you know that I can't turn them off. We need to keep everything operating smoothly, and that requires a little work. You don't understand that, but Ellen does. Look at her! Look at how seriously she takes her duty." Maxwell gestured at the image of Ellen and Kerwin.

"You're heartless."

"Having a heart is overrated. Our center proves that. Don't you agree?"

Jameson placed a liver-spotted hand over his eyes as he looked at the floor. "Just come see me in my office later."

"What? Hmmm? Oh yeah, sure, Randy. Hey, can you move out of the way? I want to get a good view of this."

After Jameson left, Maxwell returned his full attention to the screen. Jack was giving Ellen a good screw. He zoomed in. It was fun when Ellen went out on these special assignments. But he liked it even more when she came back. He was the one who owned her, not them. He knew it was smart to reward her loyalty, so he tapped a special button on his remote.

"Yes, Dr. Maxwell?" answered a secretary whose name he couldn't remember. He'd just fired the last one three days ago.

He cleared his throat. "Have Jackson select something for Ms. Standis and have it delivered to my room tonight."

"Anything specific?"

"Yes, an emerald ring." He stopped and thought. "No, a choker. Definitely an emerald choker." Maxwell imagined it around her neck as he screwed her instead of Jack.

CHAPTER 12

GAMBLING IT ALL

N ick and Melissa sat at the café table on their back patio sipping coffee. The auburn highlights in Melissa's hair glinted in the morning sun.

"You look beautiful today." Nick reached over the small table to caress her hand.

Melissa laughed. "You always say that."

"It's always true." She looked particularly stunning in her pale-blue dress with matching blazer, and he loved the sexy pumps she had on.

"Nick, are you going to be home tonight? There's something I want to talk to you about." Her tone was serious.

"So go ahead. Tell me now." He leaned back in his chair.

Melissa frowned slightly. "No, I want to wait until we have more time. It's important to me."

With mock gravity, Nick asked, "Uh-oh. What did I do?"

"Nothing, baby. I just don't want to rush our conversation."

"Okay. You sure? 'Cauz I'm already sorry, whatever it was."

"You're not in trouble." She reached over the table and kissed him impishly. Nick pulled her down and turned it into a deep, sensual kiss. He felt her give in to the pleasure. He started to thrust up her dress and pull her onto his lap.

She pushed his hands away gently. "Nick, I have an appointment."

He wasn't ready to give up yet. "Damn your appointment. When can I have an appointment? There are some things I need to discuss." He squeezed her firm ass and kissed her harder. He didn't want to wait.

Melissa pulled away from him, resting her hands on the sides of his chair and looking straight into his eyes. Her lips held a secret smile. "Tonight, I promise. After we talk."

"Well, don't forget you made me a promise, because I won't." He grabbed her hand.

"You're impossible."

"Not my fault. It's yours." Nick shrugged. He walked his eyes deliberately all over her body.

"Oh, is it? Well, I will atone for my sins later."

He grinned wickedly. "I'm going to hold you to that."

"Oh my god, Nick!" Melissa shook her head at him. "I'll see you tonight. I really have to go." She gave him a quick kiss, making sure he didn't have time to extend it. She hurried inside. He enjoyed watching her as she left.

He stayed outside on the patio. After several minutes, he heard Melissa start her car and drive away. He inhaled the fresh air and held his breath, relishing the sense of fullness in his lungs. Before he exhaled, he thought he heard something like a faint ringing sound. He jerked his head to the side, alert. In another few seconds, he realized it was the doorbell. It was an ordinary, everyday event, nothing to be concerned about. Nick left his comfortable place in the sunshine to answer the door.

A pretty woman stood before him, with pale skin, large eyes, and dark hair cut into a bob. Mid-thirties. She wore a navy trench coat with matching boots.

Nick sneered. "What the hell are you doing here?" Natalie Ricard had screwed him over once, and he wasn't going to give her the opportunity to do it again. He started to shut the door.

"Nicholas, please, it's important."

Her expression looked earnest, but Nick didn't care. "I have nothing to say to you."

"It's about Sunshine."

It was like a slap to his face. Nick blinked. How did she know he was interested in Sunshine? But no matter what information she might have, Natalie wasn't someone he could trust anymore. She'd changed. She was at least half the reason he had left the CIA. Sebastian Warner was the other half. "I don't know what you're talking about."

She looked both pained and scared. "Yes, you do. Don't play games with me. Please. You might get hurt."

"Me, play games with you? Are you serious?"

Natalie looked at the ground. "I want to help you." She raised her eyes and stared at him. She didn't seem to be lying. But he had trusted her before, and how had that worked out for him? Still...

Nick blew air out of his nostrils. He was letting his anger dominate his reason. "Fine. What about Sunshine?"

"Stay away."

Nick sighed. "I suppose you won't tell me why."

Natalie pressed her lips together. "I can't. I really can't. Just trust me."

Nick snorted. "Trust you? You are the last person I would trust. The hell with you!" He slammed the door in her face.

Inside, Nick stood with his back against the door, arms crossed. This was the second warning he'd received cautioning him away from Sunshine in as many days. In a way, it was good. Now he knew for sure the government was involved in whatever Sunshine was doing.

Nick went straight to his office to do more work on the case. He snatched a pen and a yellow lined pad from his desk and sat down in his favorite leather chair. It was worn and faded but comfortable. He tapped the pad with the pen as if he could shake ideas loose from the pages.

The way he looked at it, his task was simple. He had to determine what differentiated the children who had disappeared from those who hadn't. It was simple, actually. There was a relatively small percentage that had gone missing, so there had to be something that made them different from the others. He started jotting down possible reasons.

He spent most of the day reading through all the information he could glean from the Internet about Sunshine Children's Homes. Nothing unusual turned up. He tried to track down any known connection between Sunshine and the National Institutes of Health, but there was nothing there, either. That wasn't good. That meant that whatever they were doing wasn't something they wanted to advertise.

It had been an unproductive but busy day, the kind Nick liked least. Busy and productive was good. Lazy and unproductive once in a while was essential for his mental health. But busy and unproductive was the absolute worst. Nick was glad Melissa was going to be home tonight because that always improved his mood. Although he worried a little about the mysterious conversation she wanted to have.

When his girlfriend returned home, Nick saw immediately that her face had lost the easy brightness of the morning. The lines across her forehead were like an accusation, but Nick still didn't know what he had done. He didn't think she could have found out about his search for Sidney. At least, he hoped she hadn't.

"Are you upset, Melissa? Is it because of what you wanted to talk to me about? Should we talk now?" He kept his expression as loving as he could manage and made sure his voice was gentle.

"Um, yes. I mean no ... I mean ..." Melissa smiled weakly. "What I mean is, I would like to talk to you about something." She straightened up. "I, um, I've decided I want you to look for Sidney." Melissa's last words plunged out in a garbled jumble.

Nick wasn't sure he'd heard her correctly. "What, sweetheart?"

"I want you to look for Sidney."

Nick let his shoulders relax. "That's great, honey. But are you sure?"

"Yes, I'm sure." She was looking at him oddly again. "So when will you begin?"

Nick felt like he was being cross-examined. Uncertain, he asked, "Begin looking for Sidney?"

She enunciated, "Yes, Nick, begin looking for Sidney."

Was that what she was really asking, or was something else going on here? Had she found out and was testing him?

She raised her eyebrows and pursed her lips tightly as she stared at him.

Nick took a gamble. "Right away, sweetheart." Nick reached out to touch her.

She drew back, and her eyes narrowed. "You asshole!" she yelled. She jerked up from her chair and snatched up her purse like it was some kind of life raft. Tears tracked down her face.

Nick was alarmed. Melissa hardly ever cried. "Melissa!" he shouted to her receding back as she raced for the garage. He sped to follow her. As she slammed her car door shut he saw his suit jacket thrown across the roof of his car, the Sunshine files exposed.

CHAPTER 13

DATA ADDICTED

S taring at the ceiling, Jack couldn't sleep anymore. His body was deliciously relaxed; a slight smile gracing his face. Any man would have been smiling if he'd just been with the gorgeous Ellen Standis. She could have anyone she wanted. Why him? Pushing the question from his mind, he rolled out of bed to initiate TR. He plodded over to the office—his glass prison.

The moment he entered, those lines from the agreement about being perpetually monitored penetrated his skull like a laser. He hadn't thought of that once last night. Not for a second.

His thoughts scrambled. Had he and Ellen been filmed? Did she know? Did she care? Did she like that sort of thing? And if she did, did that turn him on or piss him off?

It doesn't matter. It doesn't matter. Like a clone, the phrase lost power with each repetition.

He didn't bother to sit down. "Start Tabula Rasa."

"Yes, Jack."

The screen came to life in front of him. All he had to do was press enter. It felt like a black hole he would be sucked into. But did the wormhole on the other side lead to someplace wonderful or terrible? He pretended it didn't matter. He pressed enter.

The second his finger lifted from the key, the Tabula Rasa interface propelled into action. The intense flow of equations on the screen was overwhelming. Jack sat down now, compelled to watch in awe.

Jack scanned line after line of heady data. He was hooked. Why hadn't he done this sooner?

Out of the corner of his eye, Jack noticed his reflection above the dresser as he passed by. He hadn't so much as glanced in a mirror for several days. He looked like hell.

He'd become a junky, addicted to the insidious glow of the Tabula Rasa monitors. He wasn't sure when he had last showered. He was certain he hadn't left his suite in days. The room service breakfast remains beside him could have been from yesterday or the day before.

Shit, how long has it been? He felt a slight compulsion to leave his apartment to prove he could, but with an addict's reasoning, he convinced himself he needed one more day in his office. *I'll sober up tomorrow, so I should indulge all I can now.* He poured a cup of lukewarm coffee from a nearby carafe.

His voice scratchy from lack of sleep, he said, "Access TR."

"Accessing."

Line upon line of material flashed on the TR computer and glowed in the dark space. Jack had stopped turning the lights on in his apartment so he could see the computer's information more clearly. Words, images, and equations lasered onto the glass wall behind him and reflected in a grid across his face. Jack sat mesmerized as he witnessed the slow, steady progress of the equations toward isolating the defective genes and reintroducing the healthy ones.

It was just a computer model, but it was clearly the work of brilliant, beautiful, insightful minds. He had never seen work so pure. It was work he was incapable of doing himself. All he had done for days was sit and watch TR's genius in action.

The haze he was in reminded him of the time in college when he had smoked pot multiple times a day for several months. He had finally stopped because it turned out he needed his mind clear to succeed in his studies. But his mind didn't need to be clear now. In fact, his mind didn't need to do anything. TR was taking care of goddamn everything. Still, he couldn't force himself away. How did they do it? And, why couldn't he talk with them?

CHAPTER 14

MAFIA AND MENSA

"How long has this place been on the market?"

Melissa blinked, turning to her client, Nancy Blair, who stared at her with raised eyebrows.

"Um, let me look." Melissa fumbled through her folder to find the information that she should've already had memorized. "One year."

Blair walked to the large glass window, her blonde hair and abundant gold jewelry glowing in the sunlight. The condominium had an amazing view of the National Mall. "So they should be willing to settle on a lower price, right?"

Melissa followed Blair's gaze out the window. Everything seemed so beautiful and calm outside. It was a perfect autumn day. Except that somebody had done something with her son, and that person was out there somewhere. Nick was out there, too, and she missed him, more than she could have imagined she would. Time away from him had made her understand what he had wanted to do for her. Why he'd lied to her.

"Ms. Ryder, I asked you a question."

"Yes, sorry. You should definitely go in lower. It's a great property, but luxury real estate has been moving slow in D.C. and there are no other interested parties right now. You have a good chance of getting it."

"Can you write up an offer?"

"Yes. Yes, of course. What were you thinking?" The part of her that spoke was like the ten percent of an iceberg above the surface of the ocean. The rest was with Sidney and Nick, regretting and—despite everything—hoping.

Rectangular folders made a pattern across Nick's large work desk that Mondrian would have been proud of. It wasn't a desk, actually, just a large slab of thick walnut secured to a trestle. Nick preferred to lay out his work this way so he could see everything at once. It was another thing Melissa teased him for.

As Nick thought of Melissa, his heart ached. It was an extraordinary feeling to him. He'd loved before, but he'd never actually missed anyone. It was a little unnerving.

He hoped she'd come home soon. She probably was staying at Victoria's until her temper cooled. She hadn't returned his calls, but that was typical when she was angry with him. That was Melissa. She'd run away from him before but had always returned. He couldn't control her, and he didn't want to. But it would be nice if she could learn to trust him with her feelings.

Activity was a good way to refocus. Nick took all the pages out of each file and arranged them according to the primary subject matter covered on that page. There wasn't much room left on the desk, just a few slivers of dark brown outlining the manila folders.

He narrowed down the categories to the mother's history, the mother's school records, foster home care, and some basic intelligence and ability tests that were run on all the babies who came to Sunshine at three, six, nine, and twelve months. There were also the children's medical records and sometimes information about the father when it was known. Then there was the pile of his own notes from his conversations with the foster families.

Got to find the common denominator. He moved the closest heap of papers in front of him, donned his reading glasses, took the cap off his pen, beginning to read.

Nick toiled through each page, underlining all statements and details that seemed repetitive. The process took a while, and frankly, it was tedious.

The first set he worked through included the mother's histories-there were lots of commonalities. Drugs, poverty, and youth were the common denominators here, but he was sure that the mothers of the children who had not gone missing had similar stories.

The process was tiresome, but this was the most important part of any investigation. He went slowly through each page and each pile because there was no way of knowing where the critical evidence would be found. He was good at this. It was a rather lackluster but valuable skill to have, and probably one of the chief reasons he'd had such a successful career in the CIA. What did that say about him? That he was boring?

Finally, he came across something that commanded his interest. Intelligence scores, whenever they were provided, were incredibly high. This was true for both the mothers and the babies. And sometimes, when there was complete information about the father, his recorded IQ was usually Mensa level.

Nick picked up Melissa's chart next. He'd intentionally avoided looking at her part of Sidney's file until he couldn't avoid it any longer. *Jesus!* She had an IQ of 185. And, she'd never told him that she had gone to all those special schools for the super-gifted. He'd known she was smart, but he'd never realized she was a genius.

Nick pulled his glasses down to the end of his nose. As bright as Melissa was, it hadn't stopped her from getting messed up on drugs. She had never turned into a true addict, so it wasn't a biochemical thing for her. Maybe it had just been a way to quiet her overactive mind at a time when it was difficult to shut off her thoughts and worries.

Nick snorted. Maybe that was why he'd never been bothered too much by his problems. He just wasn't that smart. Oh, he was smart enough to do his work well, but not IQ-of-185 smart. Maybe that made him better off. Or maybe his mind was just shooting off random bullshit.

Laughing off his mini-adventure into psychoanalysis, Nick made a list of all the intelligence scores he could pinpoint—a much more productive use of his time.

The method Sunshine had used to calculate intelligence scores for babies of three, six, nine, and twelve months utilized a test he'd never seen before. Sunshine Children's Homes, or someone who controlled them, must have developed the test. Within its parameters, all of the special Sunshine children scored significantly higher than their peers. The IQ scores of the mothers, babies, and fathers all ranged primarily from 155-195. They were occasionally higher but never lower. *Jesus.*

Nick grabbed his phone from the desk and typed the same text he had been sending Sam for days: Any identification on the subject?

Nick waited a while, but Sam didn't answer. Recently, Sam had declined to return all of Nick's calls. He might have found out that there was a connection between Sunshine Children's Homes and the man Nick had asked him to identify. Sam had made it very clear that he wouldn't have anything to do with an investigation into Sunshine.

Nick would have to find a different way to get what he needed. Taking out his black leather-bound notebook, he jotted down key points. He'd just begun to write the first item on his list when his phone buzzed. It was a text from Sam: Stay away from Sunshine. They're onto you.

Nick replied: What do you mean?

You're being followed.

That was impossible. Nick knew both how to follow people and when he was being followed. In other words, he would know if he was being followed! He wasn't. Screw Prezziato and his damn Mafia bullshit.

CHAPTER 15

IMAGES THAT DISTURB

"It seems we don't have to worry about Kerwin anymore," Scott Maxwell said from behind his desk. "He hasn't left his apartment in four days, going on five."

Ellen stared at him as she sat in the opposite chair. His round glasses framed his tiny bald head. Together they scarcely rose above his oversized desk. Maxwell was the type of man the term "Napoleon complex" had been invented for.

"That's good news."

Scott's small eyes seemed to get tinier. "You don't seem excited, Ellen."

Inwardly, she sighed. He took everything so personally. "No, I am excited. I'm sorry. I didn't sleep well last night."

Scott looked mollified. "Ah, well, that's too bad. You should visit me tonight. After I'm done with you, you'll be sure to sleep well."

She'd said the wrong thing. Taking a deep breath, she searched for a way to change his mind. Her eyes wandered to the ceiling.

"Ellen! Are you even listening to me?"

She thrust her gaze back down to meet his. "Yes, sorry. I would love to visit you tonight. That sounds perfect, Scott."

"Good, good." Something indiscernible showed on his features. In a second, she had it figured out. He was planning what he thought would be a sexy encounter later. "I'll be back in a minute. You stay right there."

Alone in his office, Ellen knew she had only a minute or two. She wanted something she could use against him to free herself from his control. She moved to his desk. He never bothered to hide anything from her. As if selecting a card from a deck, she randomly picked up one of the folders sitting on the desktop and opened it. There were photographs inside, horrible images. She gasped. What were they? Who were they? She couldn't tell.

Ellen heard Scott's footsteps outside the door and hurried back to her seat, trying to forget what she'd seen.

Jack finally emerged from his fog, feeling the urgent need to see another human face. He called Elvis and asked if they could meet at the north end café. To his relief, Elvis agreed.

When Jack arrived, the hostess informed him that Elvis was already seated. She brought him to Elvis's table.

As he sat down, Jack said, "Thanks for meeting me."

"Sure. You want some wine?" Elvis had ordered a bottle of Barolo.

"Yeah, thanks." Jack held up his glass while Elvis poured from the decanter. Jack had a taste. "Mmmm, delicious."

Elvis looked pleased with the compliment. "I'm from the region."

They made small talk until the waiter arrived, and both ordered steaks. When they were alone again, Jack said, "Thanks again for coming out. I know it isn't easy." He shot the other man a knowing look.

Elvis looked down and shook his head. "It's harder than it should be." He took a sip of the Barolo. "But I have felt a little better since talking to my group."

Jack felt a jolt of electricity travel through his brain. "You've talked to your Tabula Rasa partners? I thought they wouldn't let us."

"Yeah, well, neither did I, until recently. I pressed the issue with Dr. Maxwell, and he arranged an audio conference for me. The whole way TR works just felt so weird. I wanted to talk to the humans on the other side, you know? Their work hardly seems human at all, so I was getting a little freaked out. They're like a collection of Datas from Star Trek."

Jack laughed loudly. Too loudly. He knew it was a release of pent-up stress. "I know what you mean."

"I didn't know anyone could be that smart. And let's face it, we've been around a lot of smart people our whole lives. Jesus, I thought I was smart until recently."

Jack sipped his wine. "I think I should ask to talk to my TR team, too. It might reassure me. By the way, have you talked to the other residents about how things are going?"

Elvis shook his head. "Barely seen either one of them. I tried to strike up a conversation with Dr. Woo a few days ago at breakfast, but she didn't seem interested, and I haven't seen her since."

Jack gave a forced laugh. "Don't you remember the dirty look Woo gave you the first time we all met?"

"I was trying to give her the benefit of the doubt. Maybe she was nervous that first day, and it made her feel defensive."

"I think you're too nice. But then again this is the first time I've been out of my apartment in days, so I haven't seen anyone at all."

Elvis laughed. "I was like that at first. Pretty addictive, isn't it?"

"Yeah. It is."

Jack woke up and ordered breakfast in again, but he took a morning shower. He saw that as a good sign. He shaved, an even better sign. He felt better than he had in a week.

He put on his best suit, which was more than Dr. Maxwell deserved.

Jack took a quick walk to Maxwell's office. Just to the right of the door was the shiniest pair of black wingtips he had ever seen. They looked as if they had a coat of polyurethane on them. Jack shrugged and pressed the buzzer.

Maxwell's secretary, asked, "Who is it?"

Jack leaned close to the panel beside the door. "Dr. Jack Kerwin."

"One moment."

Jack lifted his head toward the ceiling and puffed air through his nostrils. He hated kowtowing to people who didn't deserve it.

"You can come in, Dr. Kerwin."

Jack pushed the door open. The woman behind the desk asked him to sit down, and he did. He scanned the office, which was as imposing and pretentious as he expected it to be. He picked up a newspaper on a table adjacent to his chair, but the words didn't focus into something coherent.

"Dr. Maxwell can see you now."

He felt like he was in a dentist's office. "Thank you." It wasn't her fault she worked for an asshole.

Maxwell sat behind a huge desk that made him look smaller than he was.

"Thank you for seeing me.

"What do you want?" He didn't look up.

Jack eyed a nearby chair. "Mind if I sit?"

"If you must."

Jack sat and looked at Maxwell squarely. "I would like to speak directly to my Tabula Rasa group."

Maxwell rolled his eyes. "You, too? Have you been talking to Vitali?"

"I have, yes."

"And what do you think you will learn from this interaction that you haven't already?"

Jack wasn't sure there was a good answer to that question, so he told Maxwell the truth. "I think it will make me feel better."

Maxwell guffawed. "Is that why you came to CIRAS, to feel better? Because you could feel better at a doctor's office, or a massage parlor, or at a f'ing strip club with the right girl. I didn't realize researchers came here to feel better. You have enlightened me, Dr. Kerwin." He turned his head away from Jack to stare at a wall.

"What I meant was at the end of all this I'll have the answers I wanted, but TR will still be anonymous. I just want to talk to them to understand that they're okay with that."

Maxwell's eyes flared with anger as if Jack's statement was an assault. He kept his gaze on the wall. "Believe me, they are." He pronounced each word emphatically.

"Dr. Maxwell, sir, I would still like to talk to them myself. Please."

Maxwell sighed loudly, and with what clearly took tremendous effort, he turned to look at Jack. "Fine. You can talk to them tomorrow."

"Thank you, Doctor." Jack rose from his seat.

"I hope it makes you feel better."

CHAPTER 16

ROBOTS OR REAL?

J ack pushed the button to begin the conference call. "Thanks, for agreeing to this meeting." His voice vibrated eerily off the walls of his office.

"I represent your TR group." Each word sounded distinct from the others, as though a computer spoke. Jack was curious. Were they people, computers, or a little of both?

"So the rest of them aren't there with you?"

"No."

Jack coughed. He looked down at his notes and mentally took questions that could be answered with only a yes or no off the list. "Do you have any questions about my work?"

"No."

He hadn't realized that would be a one-word answer, too. He changed tack. "I noticed that you're looking at a slightly different set of proteins then I was. Can you explain why?"

"You were using the wrong ones."

Jack clenched his fists. "Obviously, but can you walk me through it?"

"Dr. Kerwin, all of this is already on your tablet."

"Humor me."

"If I must."

"Please. But first I have another question."

"Yes?"

"Don't you mind that you never get credit for your discoveries? Why doesn't it bother you?"

"We do get credit. Everyone knows you're here, don't they? When you leave and have your template for a cure, it will be obvious that we provided the answer."

"You don't even have names."

Jack looked down at the tablet that was displaying their conversation as it happened. He took his own notes, too.

"Our name is Tabula Rasa."

"I mean individual names."

"That is the only name we care about, Dr. Kerwin."

If that were true, it was pretty bizarre. "Forget it. Let's go back to the question about the protein sequence."

"As you wish."

Jack's mouth hung open, and his head lolled forward. His body was limp. He made a strange gurgling sound. He repeated the odd iteration then suddenly jerked up straight, realizing he'd been snoring.

Jack smiled inwardly, shaking his head and rolling his shoulders backward several times, glancing up at TR's monitor. It looked the same as always. Clearly, he was no longer enthralled with sitting and watching TR work, since it was literally putting him to sleep.

He reached for his notes from the morning's phone conference and pulled up the corresponding page from the embedded tablet in his cubicle. He would have liked to be able to print from it, but that was not allowed at CIRAS.

Jack went over the questions he'd asked them this morning and their responses point by point. He was on the fifth page of notes when something stuck out. The notes indicated that TR referred to a segment of genetic code with a different label than what they had originally given this grouping earlier in the discussion. The name was similar, but it definitely wasn't the same. Why hadn't he noticed that this morning?

Jack scrolled through the last few days of TR's computations and notes. He found the label reference he was looking for, and he was right. It was not the same.

Jack checked his notes one more time. There was definitely a discrepancy. It might look minor to those who weren't in his field, but it was very important. Any label used for a gene grouping was permanent. Changing a label could mean losing track of that particular piece of the computer model, and finding it again would require dozens of hours of work to retrace steps and find the problem.

It was a rookie mistake, and it alarmed Jack considerably. He was quite awake now.

"Computer."

"Yes, Jack."

"I want you to request another meeting with my TR group." Jack leaned back in his chair with his arms crossed, expecting resistance.

"Already? You just talked to them this morning, Jack."

Jack's expression hardened. "Yeah, I know, but I need to ask them a question about something we talked about. It can't wait."

"You could ask me."

"What do you mean?"

"I mean what I just said. You can ask me."

"But I definitely need to talk to them. I mean—"

The computer interrupted him. "Just ask me, Jack."

Could a computer get angry? "Okay, fine." Jack explained the incongruity he had found between the two labels.

The computer took longer to answer than it ever had. "I understand why that would be distressing. Can you tell me the incorrect label from this morning?"

Jack read the sequence from his notes.

"Yes, that is incorrect. But maybe you are the one who made the mistake."

"I didn't make a mistake. This is all I've done for half my life, for Christ's sake!"

"Then you won't mind looking at the transcript of the conversation I just sent you?"

That made sense. "Yeah, sure. Hold on." Jack pulled it up and brought himself to the pertinent section on the tablet. "Hey." He frowned. "Hold on a second."

Jack shook his head and blinked his eyes several times. This couldn't be right. Yet, the symbols glowed with crisp distinction on the screen. The genetic label on the tablet was now the original one that TR had used. *What the hell?*

"Is there a problem, Jack?"

Jack looked up at the computer, bewildered. "What? No. I mean, I don't know. They were different, and now they aren't anymore. I don't get it."

"Well, you haven't been sleeping enough, Jack. Maybe you were just confused."

It was true that he hadn't been sleeping well. But he knew what he had seen and heard. That meant...

Jack made a quick decision. "Yeah, that must be it. Sorry to bother you."

"I am a computer, Jack. I can't be bothered."

"Yeah, right."

Jack stumbled out of the narrow opening of his office and sat down on the edge of his bed. He needed to think. He raked his hand through his hair.

What the hell was CIRAS keeping from him, from all of them? TR was just a group of people, right? They were weird people, freaky smart people, but human, right?

Jack paused. Maybe that was it. Maybe they weren't human anymore. Maybe TR members were genetically engineered, or altered, or had cybernetic components. He shuddered at the Borg-like images that intruded into his mind.

Considering the high technology CIRAS was capable of, it was feasible. Maybe all those strange metals were used for more than just sterile looking furniture. Maybe he couldn't meet with his TR group in person because then he would see for himself what CIRAS had done—how they had changed people into machines.

He made a decision to go to Jameson and see if he could get the truth from him, knowing he'd never get it from Maxwell.

CHAPTER 17

FORGIVENESS COMES TOO LATE

Nick clanked the barbell onto the rack above. His white T-shirt stuck to his chest and his light gray basketball pants were so drenched with sweat they'd turned the color of steel. The music blasting in his ears cut out, replaced by a text alert—not the one he used for Melissa. Disappointed, he frowned as he opened it.

It was just one word, an acronym. Nick stared at the word as he figured out what it implied. After a few minutes, he realized what Sam was trying to tell him, and unfortunately, it made sense. He could easily imagine the connection to Sunshine. Now he knew for sure that Warner had something to do with it. *Asshole.*

Thanks   he texted Sam then hurried to finish his workout.

Walking through the parking lot, he stopped short on his way to his car. The white Ford sedan was still there. It was the same one he'd caught a glimpse of this morning as he left the house, and again when he arrived at the gym.

It looked like Sam was right. He was being followed. But why hadn't Nick noticed until now? Maybe a new guy had taken over. Nick decided continue to view it as a good sign that he was being tailed. It meant he was making somebody very nervous.

He popped open his trunk and threw his gym bag inside. His phone buzzed. This time it was Victoria calling.

"Hey, Vic." He leaned against the back of his car. "How are you?"

"I'm fine. Nick—"

"How's Melissa?"

"She's fine, too. Nick, listen to me. Sam Prezziato has just been murdered."

Nick suddenly felt the coldness of his wet clothes against his body. "Are you sure?"

"Yes, unfortunately, I am very sure."

"Jesus! I have to go. Keep Melissa safe. She might be in danger, too. Promise me."

"Nick—"

He shouted, "Promise me!"

"I promise. Nick, just listen for a sec—"

He had already hung up.

Melissa paced up and down the length of Victoria's loft apartment. "What did he say?" she asked her friend, agitated.

"Mel, I'm sorry. Once I told him Sam had been murdered, he hung up on me." Victoria angled her spiky blond head beseechingly toward Melissa, concern filling her violet eyes. "I'm supposed to keep you safe."

"To keep *me* safe. That's ironic. What about him?"

Melissa suddenly became aware of her obsessive pacing. She forced herself to sit on a nearby ottoman. "Vic, I've screwed everything up."

Victoria contorted her wiry body and sat on the floor beside Melissa. She placed a petite hand on Melissa's knee. Melissa laid her hand over Victoria's. "Thanks for being my friend, Vic. I know I can be difficult."

Victoria flashed a subdued version of her pixie-like smile. "Not as much as you used to be. Now, when I first met you—"

"I was a cold bitch." She shook her head to fling away the memory. She didn't like to recall those days.

"No, you were just closed off. You had to work through some things before you could trust someone."

"You were very forgiving."

"And you were worth the effort."

Vic was so supportive. Always had been. Melissa wished she'd confided in her sooner. Why did she have to wait until she left Nick to open up? She wasn't going to hide the truth from her ever again. "Can I tell you something?"

"Sure."

Melissa eyed the deep purple sofa across the room. "Come sit next to me for a minute." She reached out a hand and helped Vic off the floor. They sat on the sofa together, eye-to-eye.

"You know the day I found those files from Sunshine in Nick's car?"

"Of course. You've been living here ever since."

Melissa twisted her hands together as she spoke. "I never told you that I planned on asking Nick to help me find Sidney that day. But when I saw the files in his car, I felt betrayed."

"You can't beat yourself up for that. You asked him not to investigate."

Melissa brought her hands together in a prayer-like clasp and focused on them in meditative stillness. After a few moments, she spoke again. "I need to warn him that he's in danger, and it's just as important that he knows I forgive him. I understand he was trying to help me. He knew before I did that I couldn't move on without knowing what happened."

Victoria grimaced. "I was charged with keeping you safe. I think Nick wants you to stay here." She examined the tip of her left index finger and began to chew on her nail with purpose.

"But he didn't actually say that, did he?"

"No, not exactly. But I think that's what he meant. And I don't want you to get hurt. Nick knows what he's doing. He's a professional. You aren't."

Melissa stood. "Nick is looking for my son. I should've been helping him all along. I need to go back home."

Victoria's face suggested that a battle was going on inside her. Finally, she seemed to pick a side. "Go. I love you. Please just call or text me tonight so I know everything is fine, okay?" She threw her thin arms around Melissa and hugged her.

Melissa drove so quickly and with so much internal dialogue occupying her mind that she scarcely knew how she got home. Not wanting to startle Nick with her sudden appearance, she rang the doorbell. As she waited, she rocked back and forth on her heels. She rang again. Still, there was no answer. She fumbled through her purse to find her house key and opened the door.

"Nick!" she called out, but he didn't respond. He should have been home already. Victoria said he had just left the gym. Where else could he have gone?

She went to the garage to see if his car was there. She pulled open the door. *No!* she screamed.

CHAPTER 18

ON HER OWN

Melissa regarded her fingers like they were attached to someone else as they vibrated helplessly, unable to obey her commands. She felt like she was in one of those nightmares where you couldn't get your body to do what you needed it to.

Nick lay on his back as blood pumped out of his head and from the top of his right thigh. The red liquid pooled around him in distressing quantity. Finally, she managed to control her shaking enough to dial three numbers—911.

"I need an ambulance," she tried to say, but the words were stones in her mouth. She repeated, louder this time, "I need an ambulance."

The operator asked, "What is the nature of the emergency?"

"I don't know. He's bleeding from his head and his leg."

"Who is bleeding, ma'am?"

Melissa wanted to scream at them to shut up and get here. Instead, she said, "Nicholas Sperry, my boyfriend. I think he may have been stabbed."

95

She took in a deep breath. "Please come now. We live at 22 Highland Circle in Rockville."

"We are dispatching someone now."

"Thank God."

She sank down beside Nick. Bringing her ear to his lips, she listened for the sound of his breath. It was ragged and shallow but for now, he was alive. She didn't want to leave his side, but some distant part of her mind insisted that she needed to staunch his bleeding.

Somehow she remembered Nick had just come from the gym. She opened the trunk of his car to see if his gym bag was inside, and luckily, it was. She unzipped the bag and grabbed a couple of long-sleeved T-shirts and two small towels.

She made two small square pads with the towels and placed them on each of his wounds, applying pressure. Then she took one of the T-shirts and used it as a bandage, wrapping it as many times as she could around his head to secure the pad to the wound, tying the ends of the sleeves together and made a tight knot to fasten the bandage.

She repeated the same process with what looked like a stab wound on his upper thigh. Blood immediately soaked through her improvised dressings. Melissa watched helplessly as all the white fabric turned red.

She knelt on the concrete of the garage floor and clutched her cold hand around Nick's limp one, waiting for the ambulance to come. If Nick died because he had been trying to find Sidney, she didn't know if she could ever forgive herself.

She wished so many things: that she hadn't told him about Sidney, that he hadn't wanted to help her, that she had never met him.

No, she couldn't wish that.

And with intense clarity that paralleled her intense pain, Melissa realized how forcefully she loved him. If he lived, she would tell him.

She would say the words she'd never said before. She squeezed his hand tighter, trying to forget that he might die before she had the chance.

"Ma'am, we need you to step away from him. Ma'am?"

Melissa looked about, bewildered. How long had she been waiting? People surrounded her. Who were they?

"Ma'am, you're in shock," said a man in a uniform. "Just come with us. You can ride with him in the ambulance when we know he's safe to move."

"I can't leave him." She gripped Nick's hand in panic.

A woman on her right, also in uniform, said, "We'll take care of him for you, I promise. We just need to get closer. You can wait over there." She pointed.

Melissa followed the finger and allowed other people in uniforms to take her away. She realized they were paramedics as they sat her down and took her pulse and did some other things that she didn't care about. "Please, I just want to be with him."

"You will be soon," one of them said. "They're just getting him ready so they can take him to the hospital."

"Please."

"Soon."

Somebody brought her Nick's wallet and phone. As she reached through the haze of her mind to receive the items, she thought to check Nick's phone. She tapped on messages and raised her eyebrows sharply. The last text was from Sam, and it was just one word. It must be significant.

She heard a deep male voice behind her. "I just need to ask her some questions."

"She's in shock," another male voice argued. "Can't it wait until they're at the hospital?"

"No. It can't."

Melissa heard the sounds of one human pushing another. She turned in time to see a man in a suit headed in her direction. He sat down next to her uninvited on a low bench in the garage. She had barely noticed where she was before.

A male paramedic was saying, "Leave her alone."

The man beside her took out a badge and showed it to the paramedic, then to her. It looked like a blur. Her eyes wouldn't focus right. She just wanted to get back to Nick. She needed to tell him she loved him and that she was sorry. She started to stand up.

The man with the badge said, "Sit down."

When she didn't sit down, the man pulled her back to his side on the bench. She looked at the fingers that were wrapped around her forearm. The skin beneath his grip had turned white.

"And I will need that phone." With his free hand, he snatched Nick's phone from her.

"Hey! Who do you think you are?" Melissa lurched for the phone, but he held it out of her reach.

"Just someone who wants to help you." The man placed the phone in the inside pocket of his coat. "What was Nick looking for? What had he found before he was attacked?"

Melissa sensed something in his voice. She didn't know exactly what it was, but she knew he was lying. He didn't want to help her. That wasn't what he was after. "Can you show me your badge again?" she asked. "I didn't get a good look the first time."

He took it out and showed her. He was from the CIA, just like Nick. That shouldn't worry her, but it did.

"You have nothing to be concerned about, Ms. Ryder. Can I ask you a few questions?"

Melissa sat back down. "Sure, ask away. I'll answer as best I can."

A few minutes later, the paramedic who had tried to keep the CIA man away brought her into the ambulance. It was so bright inside that she felt dizzy. She closed her eyes for a moment then opened them. The feeling passed.

The paramedic said, "You can sit next to him over here." He showed her a place on a bench.

"Thank you." She perched on the edge of it. "Is it okay to hold his hand?" Melissa looked down at Nick's inert body. He looked so different. He no longer appeared strong and in control and that frightened her.

"Of course you can. I'm sure he'll know you're there."

His words scared her, although she was sure they weren't meant to. "Is he in a coma?"

"We're not sure yet."

She choked down tears. "But he could be?"

"I'm afraid it's possible. The injury to his head and..." She stopped listening. She had already gotten the point.

Victoria sprinted into the waiting room, breathing heavily. She must have run all the way from the parking lot.

"I got here as soon as I could. How's he doing?"

"They have him in surgery now. He's stable, which is good. I was so scared he was going to die, Vic."

Victoria sat beside her—her presence, comforting.

"It's a good thing you found him."

"I know. I keep thinking what would have happened if I hadn't gotten there in time." Melissa shuddered with renewed terror, as if she were seeing it all over again. She squeezed her eyes shut.

"But you did. The important thing is that you did get there in time."

Melissa opened her eyes. "Thank God."

Victoria pulled a bottle of water out of her bag and handed it to Melissa. "Thought you might be thirsty."

Melissa eyed the water. She was thirsty but hadn't realized it. "Thanks, Vic." She unscrewed the top and took a deep gulp. She wished she could replenish the happiness in her life as easily. She prayed that Nick would heal fast and silently begged him to wake up.

"I have power bars, too, if you're hungry."

"No, thanks. I couldn't eat." She took another sip of water. As if it were a memory serum. Melissa suddenly recalled something important. "Vic, I need to tell you about the message Sam sent Nick right before he was killed. I thought it could help me figure out where to look for Sidney."

"Of course. Where is his phone?"

"Some guy from the CIA took it from me."

Victoria frowned. "That seems suspicious."

"Yeah, I know. But I remember what it said—CIRAS. C-I-R-A-S."

"No explanation?"

"No. That was it. I haven't had any time to think about what it means."

"Was Nick working on any other cases besides Sidney's?"

"No, I don't think so. I'm pretty sure he dropped them all so he could focus on finding him."

"So Sam must have been trying to tell Nick about a connection between CIRAS and Sunshine Children's Homes." Victoria sighed. "And it looks like it may have cost him his life."

Melissa felt the blood drain from her face. She was suddenly light-headed. "I got Sam killed. And Nick is in a coma because of me."

Victoria shook her head vehemently. "It's not because of you."

"But if I hadn't told Nick about Sidney, this all might not have happened." Melissa swept her gaze around the white walls of the waiting room.

"Stop. Stop it right now. You aren't helping Nick with your self-indulgent guilt. You have to be strong for him." Her words were harsh, but there was kindness in her eyes.

Melissa looked down. Victoria had a valid point. The best way to use her energy was to find out why Sam had been killed and Nick attacked. She exhaled sharply. "Okay, so what do we know about CIRAS? I thought it was some kind of think tank or something."

Victoria nodded. "It's the best one in the world. They're making amazing discoveries all the time. They're always in the news."

"What would a think tank want with babies?" As she spoke, Melissa's brain exploded with several horrible possibilities. Her mind flashed back to all those questions Sunshine D.C. had asked her about her schooling. They couldn't hide their piqued interest when she'd told them her IQ. What would a think tank do with smart babies? That was the more important question. And all of the possible answers magnified her anxiety.

"Vic, I think they took Sidney because he was very intelligent."

"What makes you say that?"

She told Victoria about the way Sunshine had interviewed her when she brought Sidney in.

"It is kind of unusual."

"What should I do?"

Victoria looked up as if an answer to her question might be dangling from the ceiling. "Whoever was after Nick, we have to assume it was because of what he found out or was on the verge of finding out. They wanted whatever that was to remain a secret. So the best way to keep him safe is to uncover that secret and tell it to the whole world."

"That sounds impossible. How am I going to do that? Nick was ex-CIA. I'm a real estate agent."

"You'll find a way. And I'll help."

"Thanks." Melissa smiled weakly. "Some pair we'll be."

101

CHAPTER 19

DEFICIT OF COURAGE

"You can see why I'm confused, Doctor."

Jameson ignored Jack's question and stared at the ground, while Jack occupied himself inspecting the room. Books bound in jewel-toned leather lined the walls, separated periodically by more sober neighbors of brown and black. The light and warmth from the flames in the fireplace softened the books' rectangular edges and imparted a sense of hominess.

Jameson looked up, interrupting Jack's thoughts. "You have reason to be wary."

"What do you mean?"

"Scott Maxwell is not a particularly kind person."

Jack couldn't help but laugh. "That's obvious. What are you trying to tell me?"

"I can't explain." Jameson contemplated the fire, looking like he wanted to lose himself in it.

Jack studied the reflection of the flames in Jameson's eyes. "Why not?"

"It would put you in more danger."

"I didn't know I was *in* danger. Talk to me, Dr. Jameson. Please."

"I can't tell you anything specific."

"There was a labeling discrepancy with my TR group. Is that something I should be worried about?"

Jameson shook his head. "No, your real group would never make that mistake."

Jack tried to keep his voice from raising. "Wasn't I talking to my real group?"

Jameson gave him a look that said explicitly, *No, you weren't.*

"Jesus F'in Christ," Jack muttered.

Jameson twisted his mouth into a half-frown and half-smile. "It makes sense for you to be upset." He turned his head away and then back, changing the subject. "I'd like to know more about Jeremy. I understand he was the inspiration for your research."

Jack was used to the question. People loved the story of how he'd gotten started in his field. Except, nobody could truly understand what it was like to lose a brother unless they had gone through it. It wasn't something you could explain. Imagine a limb, an organ, being torn from your body as you watched, helpless. That might be a close approximation. And the contrasting ways they dealt with Jeremy's death, divided him from his parents—another aching loss. They had been close before tragedy ripped them apart.

Jack crossed his arms over his chest, only answering out of politeness. "He was just like the clichés you've heard of all children who die of cancer. He was sweet, loving, kind, an inspiration to those around him." Jack paused. Jeremy truly embodied each of those adjectives. "I never could accept that he had to die, that somehow it was fine because he was such a great human being while he was alive."

Jameson raised his eyebrows. "Please, continue."

"Everyone always acts like, just because the kid is nearly an angel, it's some kind of consolation prize when he becomes one. I loved Jeremy, but I wanted him alive, with me, not to become some beautiful heart-wrenching story. Frankly, his death pissed me off. I wanted him back." He clenched the arms of the chair, looking at the floor. "I wanted my brother."

He relaxed his grip and let his arms drop, embarrassed he'd shown so much emotion.

"And that's why you came here. So other children wouldn't need to die and leave their brothers or sisters behind."

Jack nodded.

"That's the best reason that anyone has ever had. Jack, I wish…" He released a long sigh. "I'm sorry, Jack. You probably should go."

Jack could see there was no point arguing and let himself out, crossing the campus back to his apartment. He had just walked in when his phone rang. It was Ellen.

"Hey, do you mind if I come over?"

"I'm not really in the best mood."

"Maybe I can cheer you up."

"Ellen, I'm sorry. I'm so busy with work, I don't have much time."

"All I want is tonight."

Jack raked his fingers through his hair. "You sure?"

"I'm sure."

Her tone was emphatic. Jack believed her. "Okay, then come on over."

"I'll be there in ten minutes. I want to take you someplace."

"Are you sure we won't be spied on?" Jack asked as Ellen smuggled him through the wooden door.

"Not everywhere is bugged, just most places. You're lucky you're with me because I know which ones are and which ones aren't." She tilted her head sideways and parted her lips.

He found himself unable to resist. "Guess I'll have to trust you."

Ellen took his hand and pulled him all the way inside. As they entered the room, Jack recognized it was one of the surprising places of beauty found within CIRAS.

"Wait here for a minute," Ellen said. "I'll be right back." She walked behind a bamboo wardrobe screen that had a cedar hot tub in front of it.

As candles flickered, the walls blushed amber. The water in the tub flashed unpredictable reflections on its surface. The effect was intoxicating.

Ellen walked back into the room. She wore a mint-colored silk robe and gold high-heeled sandals that tied around her ankles.

"You look beautiful."

"Thank you."

"How did a place like this end up at CIRAS?"

"Dr. Jameson did it. He always hated that CIRAS had no warmth to it, so he made places like this. He designed the courtyard, too."

From what Jack had seen of Jameson's apartment that made sense. Jack pictured him as a professor at his alma mater, Harvard. He would fit better there than he did here. But he wasn't thinking about Jameson for long. "Are you sure no one saw us come this way?"

"Stop worrying, Jack. You said you'd trust me." Ellen reached around her waist to untie the robe.

Jack sank deep into the tub and allowed his entire body to relax. Ellen sat next to him, neck deep in the steaming water. "That was nice."

"Yes, it was. Thank you."

Jack looked at Ellen to try to read her expression, seemed like she was telling the truth but he couldn't be sure.

"What exactly do you do here at CIRAS besides welcome the residents?"

Ellen laughed, her voice throaty and satisfied. "That was abrupt. Do you really want to know?"

"Yeah, I do."

She seemed to stiffen up as she answered. "Officially, I'm the personal assistant to Dr. Maxwell. But I do other things too, like running a meeting here and there. And like you said, I welcome the new residents."

"Can I ask you another question?"

"Sure," she said but her mouth twitched with apprehension.

"What do you know about what is actually going on here?"

Ellen moved away from him. "What do you mean?"

"Haven't you noticed things are a little odd around here? All the surveillance and the fact that no one ever sees a single member of Tabula Rasa—isn't that strange to you?"

"I know it's a little weird, Jack. But you shouldn't question it. You really shouldn't. You might..."

He finished her sentence. "Get hurt?"

She nodded.

"I have a feeling that if I do, I won't be the first one. I think the TR members are being manipulated against their will."

Without a word, Ellen pulled herself over the edge of the tub and reached for a towel. She dried off meticulously without looking at him once.

He could tell she knew something and didn't want to talk about it. "Ellen..."

"What?" She wrapped the towel around her body and tucked in the loose end. "I was getting too hot in the tub."

"Ignoring things doesn't make them go away."

"I know. It's just that, if something is really wrong, if people are getting hurt, I don't know what we could do without..." She didn't finish. "You don't know Sco—Dr. Maxwell. He's not right. I think he might be mentally unstable."

Jack came over to her and placed his hands over her elbows. "Could we live with ourselves if we don't try to help?"

Ellen looked up at him, and he hated the answer he saw in her eyes. He was immediately less attracted to her. Without comment he kissed her lightly on the cheek, turned away, dried off, and got dressed. He felt her eyes on his back as he left.

CHAPTER 20

THE HEART OF CHANGE

Ellen studied the pretty redheaded girl who smiled up from the photo. On her left stood a stunning blonde, hair in a ponytail and a scarf around her neck. On her right was a muscular man, a football player. Her father had been a record-setting NFL quarterback before he died in a freak car accident. Ellen missed him all the time.

Her mother was another story. Ellen despised her, and they never spoke. But it seemed like she lived in her anyway—in her selfishness, and in her willingness to use her body and her beauty to get what she wanted. Her father had been focused, determined, hard-working. Why hadn't she inherited any of those qualities?

The innocuous question hurled itself into focus. She paused. Why *wasn't* she more like her father? If she was, she would be willing to help Jack, and he would never have looked at her that way—as if she had suddenly become ugly to him. She fought back the tears, trying to forget.

Ellen didn't know how long she sat motionless but gradually became more cognizant of the present. She gently closed the old photo album and hugged it to her chest. Her will rode alternating waves of capitulation and strength, and she didn't know which would take her. She wished she'd met Jack sometime in the future when she was a better version of herself.

The questions refused to go away. Was it worth trying to change Jack's opinion? Could she change simply by deciding to? Energy pulsated through her body like an electric shock as she remembered that her father had been able to do that. She'd witnessed it. He had won many football games through the sheer force of his will—as if that alone had the power to determine the outcome. A flickering notion floated through her mind, and she barely grasped it. Before it ran away from her, she hurried to her computer to type out a letter. She'd tell him everything. Confession. Then atonement.

Branches blurred past. The earth felt good under Jack's feet, and his heart raced with an intensity that let him know he was alive. Residents at CIRAS were allowed to use designated paths around the property, and they were perfect for his morning runs.

The mid-November air chilled his nostrils and lungs, invigorating him. He missed the outlet of competition and promised himself that he would find a way to play soccer in a league again. There were some good ones around with players just like him who could have gone pro but had other things in their lives that were more important than soccer.

Jack turned his head toward the sun as he headed down a path beside a stream. The dappled sunlight on the water reminded him that there was a world that existed outside of CIRAS. For about a month now, his work with TR had been so consuming that he had almost forgotten. Breathing in, he returned his gaze to the path and settled into a steady stride.

While his body was occupied with the task of running, his mind returned to Ellen, as it had again and again over the past few days. What did she know? Had he been too hard on her? He didn't like the way she had responded to his questions. Then again, sometimes he could react one way initially, but in time he would come around. Maybe Ellen was like that, too. Maybe he had overreacted. *Yeah, or maybe it's your libido talking.* He snorted. That was a real possibility. He ran faster and whipped around a corner. After a few more fast-paced minutes, he started to sweat.

Jack did like her, or he thought he did. It was hard to tell because she was so unbelievably sexy and that clouded his judgment for sure. Then he remembered how unattractive she had seemed when she wouldn't talk to him about what was wrong with CIRAS. He amped up his pace.

He didn't know what he thought. *I should just talk to her again.* His conscience prodded. Or maybe it wasn't his conscience at all.

Sweat dripped down every centimeter of his body. He ran harder than he had in a long time but couldn't sideline his thoughts. He finally gave up, got out his phone, and called her. "Hey, Ellen. Meet me for dinner tonight?"

"Jack, I can't. You know how things are around here."

"No, actually, I have no idea what's going on around here," he yelled, not meaning to. He took a quick gulp of air to calm down. "I'm not going to let it control my life. What's the worst they can do?"

Ellen paused. "You really want me to answer that?"

"Okay, fine. I see your point. But Jesus, Ellen, I'm not going to live like a caged animal. Do you want to meet me for dinner or not?" His delivery was harsher than he intended.

Ellen hesitated before she said, "Yes."

Ellen spun around to greet Jack at the entrance to the restaurant and in that single moment he was undone. She wore a slim-fitting, green turtleneck sweater and black leather pants and boots. Jack walked up to her and kissed her on the cheek. "You look unbelievable."

She bit the side of her lip. "And you look very handsome, Jack."

"Thanks. Want to get a table by the window?"

Ellen nodded. "That would be perfect." Her energy seemed subdued. She was probably thinking about their last encounter and how it had ended. He hadn't forgotten it, either.

They were seated and ordered cocktails and a couple of entrees. Ellen sipped her martini but hardly ate anything. Jack concentrated on his burger and Guinness.

Ellen set down her empty martini glass and ordered another. "So, Jack, what sorts of things do you do for fun?"

Jack raised his eyebrows and swallowed his bite. "For fun?"

"Yes, for fun. You can't possibly work all the time." She correctly interpreted his expression. "Can you?"

Jack shrugged his shoulders. "Pretty much."

The server brought Ellen's martini and set it before her. She smiled and thanked him before turning back to Jack. "Well, I know you work out." She winked at him. "I can tell."

"Yeah, I work out. And I used to play a lot of soccer."

Ellen perked up. "What position?"

"Goalie."

"Do you ever think about getting back into it?"

He smiled. "It's funny you should ask that..."

They talked for an hour. Ellen was a great conversationalist, and if Jack could have forgotten where they were, it would have felt like they were on a date. Despite his misgivings about her seemingly selfish nature, he wanted her now, and badly. He stared at her and sighed at his own hypocritical nature.

Ellen tilted her chin and looked at him sideways like she was trying to figure something out. She asked, "Am I annoying you?"

Jack was confused. "Why?"

"You just sighed like you were exasperated."

Jack laughed. "Only with myself."

"I know what that feels like." She smiled softly and looked defenseless, which intrigued him.

"What do you mean?"

She pulled at the cuffs of her sweater. "Oh, what you were talking about the other night just got me thinking. It made me look honestly at some of the choices I've made. I'm not proud of a lot of them. And I'm still having trouble changing."

"That sounds like you're a normal human being to me. Even when you see something you want to change, that doesn't mean it's easy to do."

Ellen drew her eyebrows together. "How do you know so much about people?"

Jack joked, "I don't know if you noticed, but I am one."

Ellen ran her eyes up and down his body. "Oh, I noticed."

Jack blushed. He reached across the table and wrapped his hands gently around hers. "I believe in you, Ellen. I believe you can become whoever you want to be—someone who is beautiful both on the outside and the inside."

Ellen looked like he had just slapped her across the face. "You don't know anything about me, Jack." She pulled her hands from his grasp. Her eyes shone with tears as she reached into her bag and pulled out a letter. She handed it to him with a trembling hand. "See if you still think that after you read this." Then she stood up and fled.

CHAPTER 21

MELISSA'S TURN

M elissa closed the drawer of Nick's bedside table, sighed, and went over to his closet. "Have you found them?" she called out to Vic, who was in the bathroom.

"No, nothing. You having any luck?"

Melissa frowned. "No. I wonder where he put them." She stared at his suits.

Victoria walked into the closet. "Nick wanted to hide them from you. Where would he think was a good place?"

Melissa smiled a little. "Perfect question."

She suddenly noticed the dark circles under her friend's eyes and the grayish pallor of her skin. "Thanks for helping me, Vic."

"I don't mind. I want to. Now, what was your good idea?"

"Follow me."

Melissa led the way into the basement, Victoria close behind. She and Nick had organized it last winter, so it was easier to get around now. Surveying the area, she found what she was looking for. "Over there." She pointed to a large collection of camping equipment in the corner.

Victoria gave her an incredulous glance. "You and Nick camp?"

Melissa couldn't help but giggle. "No, just Nick. Hunting, boy stuff, you know. Anyway, he usually hides my Christmas presents in here. So maybe ..." She started shifting things around. Victoria jumped in to help.

"Do you always snoop?"

"What?" Melissa picked up a large backpack and looked inside. It was empty, so she set it back down.

Victoria lifted a large canvas tarp. "Do you always look for your Christmas presents?"

"Usually. Is that bad?"

"No. I just never knew that about you. You seem so proper."

Melissa smirked. "I haven't always been. Guess I'm just a mash of contradictions." She found a cooler and opened it - old Budweiser cans but no files. Repressing a sigh, she moved on to the next pile of junk.

She lifted up some sleeping bags. When she saw the tote bag filled with folders and notebooks her heart began to pound. And when she recognized Nick's scribble on the pages she thought it might leap out of her chest and run away.

She wished that she hadn't been so stubborn, and it was hard not be consumed with anger at herself. But she had found the folders and Nick's notes, so she could try to further the progress he had made and give his sacrifice some meaning—and maybe save the lives of some children in the process.

Melissa asked, "Do you mind helping me bring this stuff upstairs?"

Vic looked at the large bag. "I bet it's heavy. How about we each take a handle and carry it up that way?"

Melissa picked up the right side and Victoria the left. They went right into Nick's office and plopped the tote on the wood floor.

Victoria suggested, "I can look at the files, and you can start with the notebooks."

"Okay." Melissa picked up the notebooks and sat in Nick's favorite leather chair. It made her feel closer to him.

Opening up the first one, she found a chart of foster children that all had incredibly high IQs, just like she suspected. She flipped the page—more of the same.

"Hey, Mel, come look at this." Victoria was seated at Nick's desk with an open file in front of her.

Melissa moved behind Vic and looked over her shoulder. The name *Sidney Ryder* was stamped across the top. " Oh my God. I need to sit down." She staggered back to Nick's chair and fell into it, clutching her knees against her body.

Vic read through the file aloud. Finally, she reached the part Melissa dreaded. "The mother left the child alone overnight. When she returned—"

Melissa interrupted. "That's enough." She covered her eyes with her hands. "I can't hear anymore."

"Melissa, there's something else in here, some notes that Nick took. Apparently, he visited some families who fostered the targeted children."

"Was Sidney one of them?"

Victoria shuffled through the papers. "Yes."

"Let me see."

She handed Melissa the sheet without comment.

Melissa glanced over it rapidly. "The Walkers. I have to go, Vic." She rushed out of the room.

Victoria ran behind her as she skidded into the garage. She'd forgotten that the bloodstains were still there, and she closed her eyes for a moment, forcing herself not to cry. Then they were in Nick's car and pulling onto the highway. She couldn't think, evaluate, or decide. She just needed to do. It was the only thing that kept her from breaking down and sobbing.

As they drove, Victoria asked, "Are you sure you're ready for this, Mel?"

"How could I ever be ready? But I have to. Maybe they can tell me something about Sidney."

"I'm sure they can. But realize that they probably aren't aware of what happened to him."

Melissa stared through the windshield, driving as if on autopilot. "I know. But they could tell me if his eyes stayed blue, what color his hair was, if he smiled a lot, when he crawled and walked, when..." Melissa sniffed. "I'm sorry."

Victoria clasped a tiny hand over Melissa's knee. "There's nothing to be sorry about."

Melissa's phone rang.

"Do you want me to see who it is?"

Melissa nodded.

Victoria pulled the phone out of the cup holder. "Answering for Melissa Ryder." She listened for a moment and then said, "Mel! Go to the hospital now! Nick might be waking up."

CHAPTER 22

AN UNLIKELY ALLY

Melissa looked up at the doctor. "You said he was coming out of his coma." Disappointment threaded through each syllable.

"The signs were there. I'm sorry. We'll let you know if anything changes."

"Thanks."

Victoria said, "Oh, Mel. I feel terrible. This is awful."

Melissa had too much emotion roiling inside to be able to talk about it. "Do you mind if I have some time to myself? To process things?"

"We don't need to talk. I could just be here."

"I know. I kind of want to be alone."

Victoria nodded as she rose from her chair. "I understand. Call me if anything changes with Nick, okay?"

"Of course." She gave Victoria a quick kiss on the cheek. "Thanks for coming."

Someone slipped into the seat next to Melissa, which was odd because all the others were empty. She glanced and saw the hint of a pretty face and a dark brown bob. The woman looked European.

"Hi, Melissa." The woman said her name as if she knew her. "I can help you help Nicholas."

Melissa tightened up. It might have been her nerves, but she found herself looking around for something to use as a weapon.

"You need to get him off his IVs and out of the hospital." She spoke quickly and quietly and darted her eyes about as she explained.

The woman was crazy. "What?"

"Nick's coma is drug-induced, and his injuries are fairly minor. I have good reason to believe that once he's off the drugs, he will recover quickly."

"Who the hell are you? And even if you're right, how am I going to get him out of here?"

"Like I said, I'll help."

"How?"

"I work for the CIA."

"Great." Melissa stared at her. "I don't trust everyone who works for the CIA. In fact, it counts against you."

"Then you're a smart woman. But, you can trust me. I promise. I care for Nick very much."

Melissa pursed her lips. Nick had had a girlfriend who also worked for the CIA. And, she definitely couldn't be trusted. "Natalie?" The woman nodded. "Nick despises you."

Natalie looked as if she had been struck. "I know. I did what I did to to save his life."

"That's not what Nick said."

"He doesn't know the whole story." Nick's ex-girlfriend leaned in closer until her mouth was an inch away from Melissa's ear. "It might not be safe to talk here. Can we go to your car?"

How could she trust the woman who had been one of the primary reasons Nick had left the CIA? Melissa stared ahead, not knowing how to answer.

"You can listen to what I have to say, and if it doesn't make sense to you, you can decide not to do anything."

"Fine." Melissa snatched her purse off the chair.

The night was incredibly cold for late November. As they crossed the parking lot, Melissa saw a few stars overhead that defied the noisy light of the city. It felt like they were lying to her.

Melissa unlocked the car. They slid inside, and she started it up. Turning on the heat, she faced Natalie. "Convince me."

Natalie pulled a lock of loose, dark hair around one pale ear as she sighed. "Long version or short?"

"Short. But don't leave out anything important."

As Natalie spoke, Melissa considered everything she now knew about secret government projects. Ten minutes later, she had to admit that Natalie's story was believable. She'd let Nick think she'd run an NIH project to experiment on prisoners just so he wouldn't try to expose it and get himself killed. He'd kept quiet to keep Natalie from a life sentence. He'd hated her ever since.

After her carefully designed attack, Natalie conspired to put Nick in an induced coma but it was only a stalling technique. Eventually, they'd want him dead. Just like she had in the past, Natalie had done what was necessary to keep Nick safe, even though she risked her job and perhaps her life to do so. Would Nick have stayed with Natalie if he'd known the truth? Melissa didn't want to know the answer to that question. If she and Nick got through all this together, there was no way she could give him up at the end of it, no matter how worthy the competition.

His ex-girlfriend insisted she could get Nick released from the hospital and transferred to a place where he could stay until he woke up. Natalie could also provide a nurse who could be trusted to take care of him for as long as necessary.

Natalie, Natalie, Natalie. Melissa didn't want to be indebted to Nick's old girlfriend, who still cared for him so much she was willing to put everything on the line. But she didn't have a choice if she wanted to save Nick.

Melissa was supposed to meet the paid-off ambulance guy and the nurse here, and then she would take Nick to Natalie's safe house. It felt like she was in a nightmare, or a horror movie. She breathed deeply to calm herself, but it didn't change how she felt.

The ambulance driver brought Nick out of his truck. He was strapped into a wheelchair and slumped forward from the chest up. Melissa could see he had been secured to the wheelchair beneath his blankets. Other than the area between chest and hips that was fastened to the chair, he was limp and lifeless. His bandaged head sank to his chest, and his arms hung at his sides. He looked worse than he had lying in his hospital bed, where at least he appeared to be resting. Now he looked like a corpse. Melissa shivered and shook herself back to the moment.

A Hispanic woman said to Melissa, "Hi, I'm Sonya Suarez, Nick's nurse."

She responded absently, "Hi."

"Are you able to help me get Nicholas into the car?"

Nicholas. Who called him Nicholas? "Yes. Just tell me what to do."

They worked to maneuver Nick into the car. They banged his limbs several times and nearly dropped him twice. Melissa felt sure that was due to her inexperience. She'd personally increased his injury tally by at least several more bruises and maybe an abrasion or two. Finally he was fastened into the seatbelt, and she slid beside him, holding his unresponsive hand.

Suarez jumped into the front seat, starting the car. She punched the accelerator, and Nick's unconscious body lurched forward with frightening ease, looking eerily like a crash-test dummy.

"Be careful!" Melissa screeched, simultaneously wondering if by taking Nick out of the hospital she was putting him in more danger instead of less. His vulnerability was palpable, and it terrified her. Why had she believed Natalie? Maybe she was just using her to get rid of Nick, not help him. Why hadn't she thought of that before?

No, calm down. Natalie's explanations had been too complex and made too much sense to be lies. Nobody could be that good at deception. She hoped.

"Melissa, things are going to be okay," the nurse said. "I will help Nicholas get better."

"How do you know that?" she screamed. Her reaction frightened her, making her burst into tears. She hid her face against Nick's shoulder but he couldn't soothe her tears, which made her cry even harder.

CHAPTER 23

UNITED FORCES

J ack brooded as he gazed through the glass wall, keeping one hand molded around his cup of coffee while tapping the other on the café table.

Reading Ellen's letter sent his emotions and his reasoning power careening in opposite directions. He was left stranded on an island in between, not knowing how to escape.

He was impressed with the courage required to be that honest. But maybe, he thought, Ellen had been too honest. It couldn't just be about sex anymore. It was way more complicated than that. And, he cared about her. She deserved his honesty, though it seemed she thought differently.

Vitali entered the cafe, stopping in front of his table. "Mind if I sit down?"

Jack tore his mind away from his thoughts. "Sure."

Elvis knit together his rather abundant eyebrows and peered at him. "You sure? You look like you might want to be alone."

Jack huffed. "I definitely don't want to be alone." Hearing the irritability in his voice, he added, "Please sit down. Sorry. I'm acting like an ass."

Elvis seated himself with his coffee and a donut in hand. "Want to talk about it?"

"Nope, and I don't want to think about it, either. Which is why I don't want to be alone. So help distract me. What's up with you?" Jack sat back and absently took a sip of lukewarm coffee.

"Not much." After a pause, he asked, "What do you think about what happened to Dr. Jameson?"

"What? I haven't heard anything."

"He got carted off to the loony bin." Elvis took a bite of his donut and chewed slowly.

"Are you kidding?"

"I'm dead serious. They say he had some kind of breakdown, and Maxwell had him taken to a high-security psychiatric center for his own protection. Jameson can't have visitors or anything. It's so sudden." He lowered his voice and leaned closer. "Kind of fishy if you ask me."

The man Jack met was definitely sane. He might have had convoluted notions of right and wrong, but he was both smart and lucid. Jack would bet his life on that.

From the moment those blue lasers at CIRAS's entrance scanned him, Jack was on guard. Now he was on high-alert—his heart beating more rapidly, his pulse racing. Defiance surged, and he wanted to ignore it, but it wouldn't subside. Whoever was running the TR project, it wasn't Jameson. Otherwise, he wouldn't have been committed. That left Maxwell - the weirdo who employed Ellen as a highly paid prostitute and spy - Jack still hadn't wrapped his mind around that one completely.

She'd explained that growing up her mother had never been satisfied with their income. No matter how much her father made, she wanted more. When she looked at the teenage Ellen, she hadn't seen a daughter but an opportunity. Ellen had been forced to date older men and extract presents from them that her mother had wanted for herself—money, cars, jewelry, even vacation homes. Maxwell had started out as one of those men. First she manipulated him with sex. Later, he'd wanted her to manipulate others. But he'd also been the one to free her from her mother's control. It was complicated.

"Um. Jack?"

"Huh?" Jack's focused back on Elvis, who looked troubled. "Sorry, I was in my own head."

"Guess I'm not being a very good distraction."

Jack ran a hand through his hair. "It's better anyway. Ignoring it isn't going to help anyone."

Elvis appeared completely confused. "Good luck figuring it out."

"Luck would be good. Might be the only thing that will work."

Jack's concern for his personal safety was blurred by his need to end whatever madness was occurring at CIRAS. Jameson had essentially been imprisoned. That was the truth. Ellen was trapped into working for Maxwell. The researchers were being controlled and spied upon. And the TR members were clearly being manipulated, and maybe even hurt or killed. Jack vowed to save whoever he could, however he could.

The worst feeling he'd ever experienced was his total impotence against Jeremy's disease. He raged against experiencing that feeling again, and if it cut him off from nature's inherent program of self-protection, then good. That would make everything a lot easier.

Carried on a wave of indiscriminate emotion, he headed to Ellen's apartment to give her his answer.

It opened widely before him. Ellen stood there in only her underwear.

Feeling a strange mix of frenzy and lust, he asked, "How did you know it was me?"

Ellen opened her mouth. "I..."

Jack looked sharply at her and narrowed his eyes, the truth assaulting him. "You didn't know it was me." He enunciated each word slowly and turned his back to walk away. His mother had trained him to be kind to women, but his patience wasn't endless.

"Wait!"

Jack spun around. "Tell me why I should."

Ellen gulped. "I deserve that."

"Yes, you do. But you still haven't given me a reason to stay. In fact, I'm leaving now." Jack fumed as he stalked down the hall. He heard Ellen following him.

"Jack, stop!"

He kept his back to her and continued walking. "I'm sorry, but I have nothing to say to you. You wrote me you weren't going to sleep with him anymore. I know you don't owe me anything, but I don't like liars. I've been honest with you about everything, and I expect honesty in return." He added sarcastically, "If that's not asking too much."

"Jack, I understand why you're angry, but it's complicated, and this isn't just about me and you. I don't care what you think about me. I mean, I do, but that's not the most important thing right now. I want to help, I really do. I want to help you stop what's going on here, just like I said in my letter. Can you at least come inside so we can talk about it?"

Jack turned and looked at her. She still wore only her underwear. He let his silence speak for him. His chest heaved up and down, and his temper threatened to take over.

"Please, just listen."

"Fine but put some clothes on." He gestured her back toward her apartment. When they got inside, she signaled for him to wait a minute. She returned dressed in sweats and a t-shirt then went into the bathroom, turning on the shower and sink faucets. Then all the lights went off. She must have done that, too. He had to admit it was a good idea.

Ellen gripped his shoulder in the darkness and led him into the bathroom. He didn't object as she guided him to sit on the floor beneath the dome of privacy created by the running water. "Smart," he said.

"Something I saw in a movie."

Jack grunted in response.

"Thank you for coming inside."

"You were dressed for *him*, weren't you?"

"Yes. But..." Ellen sighed. "Jack, I'm not even going to try to explain. But I meant what I said in my letter and out there in the hall. I do want to help. I saw some photographs from the TR Center and couldn't exactly make out the figures in them, but what I could see looked horrific." Her voice caught. "I know something really bad is happening here. You made me realize I couldn't live with myself if I didn't try to help."

Jack remained silent.

"I know you're upset with me. I don't blame you." She slid her hand onto his thigh, and he tensed up. Her caress was like a jolt of electricity, pain and pleasure at once. "But I know more about how to get around this place than Sco... Dr. Maxwell thinks I do. I promise I can help. You just have to let me."

Why did she have to go ahead and touch me? It was so unbelievably distracting. "You're right." Ellen's hand relaxed further onto his thigh. He felt like he was burning up beneath her touch. "I came here to take you up on your offer for help. Sorry I got angry with you. What you do with your body is your business."

"I don't want to be with Scott."

Forcibly ignoring the effect she had on him, Jack said, "So that's why you came to the door to greet him half-naked?"

"I was just buying time."

Jack scoffed. "What are you talking about?"

"He asked me to go see him, and I hadn't responded yet. I think he suspects I like you. He doesn't ask me to go to him that much anymore, but he gets strangely jealous sometimes.

"When I heard the banging on my door, I thought it was Scott. And I thought if I had, um, fewer clothes on, he wouldn't be so angry anymore. It was all I could think of at the time. I'm sorry, Jack."

Jack felt a little bit like an ass. She hadn't asked him to come into her life, and she had already been involved with Scott for so long that she might not be able to stop the relationship right away without putting herself in danger. Neither of them really knew what the man was capable of.

"I'm sorry."

"Like I said, I don't blame you. You didn't know what you were getting into when you came here and met me. I'm the one who should apologize."

Ellen slid her body closer to his so their thighs touched and the edge of her elbow pressed into his waist. She continued to grip his thigh lightly. With a lot of effort, Jack ignored her proximity.

"Think about it, Jack. Think about it objectively. If Scott even suspects that I'm helping you expose whatever he's doing here, I become much less useful. I have no choice but to play along with him while we investigate."

The pitch-dark room was full of hot steam and the sounds of gushing water. It was all very sexy and Jack was having a hard time of it. She was right. And she was so close... He reached for her shoulder, found her neck instead, and pulled her on top of him. She gasped in surprise, then relaxed on top of him. The floor of the bathroom was cold and hard, but Ellen's body was soft and delicious.

"Jack, I want this." She pressed herself against him. "But I want to stop Scott even more, whatever he's doing. I don't want to confuse the two."

"We don't have to confuse the two. I know I want both." He went to kiss her.

She pulled back. "Are you sure? You know what I've been to Scott. I'll help you whether you want to be with me or not. I'll understand either way." The words sounded like they were difficult for her to say.

"I'm sure."

CHAPTER 24

LESSER EVILS

A t the safe house, Suarez bustled about to get Nick's room ready. As Melissa sat beside Nick, she watched the nurse laying out the IV bags and syringes she would need to sustain him while they waited for the coma-inducing drugs to wear off.

She gazed down at her boyfriend's supine body and sighed heavily then looked up at Natalie, who stood nearby, waiting to help move him into the other room. She felt reluctant to express gratitude toward the woman, even though it was warranted. Still, it was the right thing to do. "Thank you for all this." She gestured toward the interior of the safe house. "You didn't have to. Aren't you afraid you'll get caught?"

Natalie looked over at Nick. "He wanted to do the right thing years ago, and I stopped him because I thought I had to keep him safe. He deserved to make that choice for himself. I made a mistake. It's worth it to make up for that."

"I can understand that. I'm just so worried about him."

Sonya, who stood a few steps away from them, offered a smile to Melissa. "Don't worry soon he'll be as good as new. It's time to move him into the other room. Are you ready?"

Melissa and Natalie looked at each other and nodded.

It seemed a little easier moving Nick this time, but not by much. Melissa wondered more than once if an unconscious person bruised easier than a conscious one. She felt scared and guilty and helpless. Her palms were clammy, and her heart raced in time with her worrying thoughts.

Afterward, Natalie went to put on a pot of tea, but Melissa stayed in the room and watched as Sonya connected Nick's IVs and attached a frightening number of monitors to him. His body was surrounded by and pierced through with various tubes and wires as if caught in some futuristic trap.

A picture of Sidney hooked up to various lines, his brainpower manipulated by a CIRAS machine, cast itself unbidden into her mind. Melissa closed her eyes to expel the image.

Sonya appeared competent as she moved around Nick, although Melissa admitted to herself that she wouldn't know the difference if Sonya was instead doing something that would hurt him. There was no way to discern if the liquid in those clear plastic bags hanging on hooks was poison or life-sustaining fluid. Time seemed to slow as she continued to watch. Worry captured her in its grasp and paralyzed her.

Victoria put a soft hand on her arm. "You look a little spooked."

Melissa looked at her and blinked as if she had just woken up. "When did you get here?"

"Just a couple minutes ago. Melissa, you don't have to put your brave face on for me. In fact, I don't want you to. Please."

"Thanks," Melissa whispered. She clung to Victoria's small frame. "Suppose Natalie is wrong? Suppose he dies anyway?"

"He's not going to die."

"You don't know if that's true, Vic. None of us knows if it's true."

"I do." Sonya turned and stared unwaveringly at Melissa. "He is not going to die, because I won't let him. In fact, he should be awake in twenty-four hours or so."

"See." Victoria gave Melissa's shoulder a firm squeeze. "Come and sit down with me for a little bit."

Melissa stared at her helplessly. She felt untethered without Nick. She had never realized...

Victoria must have seen the look on her face. "Okay, I admit, it might not help, but come sit down anyway. You can't help by staring at him." Victoria turned Melissa away with a gentle push.

She allowed her friend to pivot her around and lead her into the living room. Natalie was seated on the sofa, but she didn't look settled in. She looked as uncomfortable as Melissa felt.

There was a tray with tea service on the coffee table looking out of place.

"Can I pour you two some tea?" Natalie asked.

Melissa looked down. She didn't like that Natalie was here, even though her help was essential. And Natalie clearly felt awkward around her, too.

"Or maybe wine would be better."

Victoria raised her eyebrows and glanced at Melissa. "That might not be a bad idea. Just a glass or two?"

Melissa shrugged. "Sure, okay."

Sonya poked her head into the room. "Just wanted to let you ladies know I'm going to lie down for a little while. Nicholas is stable, but I'll be close by if you need me for anything."

Natalie said, "Thanks, Sonya."

"Are you the one who calls him Nicholas?" Melissa asked Natalie sharply. It had just occurred to her that was probably why Sonya always said "Nicholas" instead of "Nick." It bugged her. A lot. It was like she had a claim on him that Melissa didn't.

Natalie's eyes held no malice as she answered. "Yes, I am. Nicholas was my father's name. He was Greek. I guess I just got in the habit of using his full name because nobody ever called my father Nick. It felt unnatural to me. I don't mean anything by it, Melissa. Nicholas—I mean, Nick—and I were over a long time ago."

She seemed to be telling the truth. "But you said you still care about him."

"I do. But that doesn't mean I want to be his girlfriend again. I just don't want to see him die." Natalie made a strange face that Melissa couldn't interpret. Then Natalie stood up and lifted the tea service off the coffee table. "Let me switch this out for us. I definitely think we'll do better with wine. And Melissa—" Natalie looked at her pointedly. "I promise I'll answer any questions you ask. I know you probably have a lot of them."

"I'll come help," Victoria called after Natalie as she walked into the kitchen.

Melissa was left alone in the living room with her scrambled thoughts. They were unpleasant company, and she was sick of having them around. She wished she had a switch in her brain that would shut them off for a little while. Maybe the wine would help. She hadn't had a glass in ages.

From the kitchen, Victoria asked, "Red or white?"

"Red, I guess."

"Pinot noir or Cabernet?"

"Do you think I care?"

"No. Sorry."

Melissa wasn't able to take Natalie up on her offer to answer questions until she was halfway into her third glass of wine. "So who attacked Nick? Was it someone from the CIA?"

"Melissa..."

"Just tell me."

"It was me."

Melissa stared. "You!" She lunged at her.

Natalie quickly had her in a hold she couldn't escape. *Must be some freaking CIA thing*, Melissa thought.

"Let me explain. Please."

Victoria intervened. "It can't hurt to listen, Melissa."

"Why should I? She nearly killed him!"

"I was supposed to kill him. I didn't. Melissa, understand I was sent to murder him. I had to make it look believable and keep him alive at the same time. I volunteered. If they had sent someone else, the job would have been done cleanly and efficiently. That's why I offered to do it myself."

Melissa felt like she had been knocked out. "All that blood. You needed to make him bleed that much?"

"That was intentional. The injury to his thigh hit an artery that produces vast quantities of blood but isn't fatal if you stop the bleeding in time. And his head injury was essential. How could I convince the CIA to authorize coma-inducing drugs if he didn't already have trauma to his head?"

Melissa was stunned. It all made sense, and at the same time it was unbelievable. She didn't want to trust Natalie, but she did anyway. She slugged down the rest of the liquid courage in her wine glass. "Do you know what happened to my son?"

Natalie turned her way-too-pretty face toward her. "I begged off the CIRAS project because I could see the direction it was going. I didn't want to be involved. So, in answer to your question, no, I don't know exactly what Scott Maxwell did to the children from Sunshine. I never had full clearance on that project. Only a couple of people ever did."

133

Melissa could feel the effects of the wine, but she wasn't drunk. She understood and believed Natalie's explanation. "Thank you."

"I want to help you and Nick, and I want CIRAS shut down. But I can't be directly involved. Nick will have to take over when he's well enough. If I get caught…"

"You might end up like Sam Prezziato," said Victoria.

Melissa flashed a quick look at Victoria. She had almost forgotten Vic was there. "Yes. We can't let that happen to you, Natalie. Too many people have been hurt already. Just tell me what I need to do, and I'll do it."

Natalie pressed her lips together. "You're a strong person. I can see why Nicholas, I mean Nick, wants to be with you."

Before Melissa could answer, she heard sounds of stirring coming from the other room.

CHAPTER 25

NATALIE EXPLAINS

N ick wanted to turn over, but pain forbade it. He groaned. Where was he? His body was restrained, tangled up in strange cords. He needed to escape, but again the pain said no.

His body felt weak, his throat abnormally dry, and his vision was blurry. He closed and opened his eyes methodically to try to bring them into focus, but he couldn't see any clearer. Where the hell was he?

"Nick, it's okay." The face that hovered over him looked like a muted interpretation of Melissa's. Attempting to speak, his voice came out in a harsh, painful whisper.

"Get him some water!" *Melissa's voice.*

The image of her face resolved. "You're safe. Just relax."

"What..." The parched word crawled out of his mouth.

A faucet was turned on and water gushed. It sounded abnormally loud. Soon after, Victoria hurried into the room with a full glass. It sloshed over the sides as she hurried toward him.

"Here." Victoria thrust the glass toward Melissa.

She brought it slowly to his lips with one hand as she used the other to lift his neck. He felt so feeble and was surprised how much he needed her help. He still hadn't figured out where he was or what was going on. He took a couple sips of water and rested, then took a few more. He tried to pull more oxygen into his lungs. With each breath, his vision and memory clarified.

Melissa looked different. There was something about her that was not as he remembered her. What had happened? *Think harder. Inhale. Exhale. Inhale. Exhale.* She was beautiful. She was always beautiful, but she definitely had changed in some way. *Inhale. Exhale. Inhale. Slow exhale.* There was something in her eyes that had never been there before. What was it?

"I love you, Nick." She had never said those words. He tried to smile, but his lips were too dry and they cracked. He tasted blood on his tongue. "I love you too, baby."

She leaned down and kissed him. The warmth and wetness of her kiss banished his discomfort making him wish he could be alone with her, someplace else. Home. Anywhere. Not here.

Where was here?

"You're probably wondering where you are."

He nodded, trying to straighten up a little.

Melissa looked at him sternly. "I'll tell you, but you need to promise to be a good patient and lie still."

"Yes, nurse." He tried to grin.

Melissa smiled, but her eyes glistened with tears. "Still irrepressible."

"Always. Can I have a little more water please, nurse?"

She lifted the glass off the table beside him and brought it to his lips.

"Only give him a little bit at a time, or he won't keep it down," Sonya warned as she walked into the room and positioned herself at Nick's side. "I'm going to have to have some time alone with my patient," she said to Melissa and Victoria. "I will let you know when I'm done."

"Can't I just stay in the room?" Melissa asked. "I'll sit over there." She pointed to a chair in the corner.

Sonya agreed but shooed Victoria out.

Nick sighed. He was sore everywhere. As the nurse ran various tests on him and Melissa watched, Nick relived the night in his garage.

When he'd returned from the gym that night, Natalie was waiting for him. He'd had no time to react. Her eyes were seas of guilt as she said, "I'm sorry," and shot him with something that paralyzed his body and knocked him unconscious. His injuries must have been inflicted after that.

He could feel that the top of his right thigh and his head were bandaged heavily. His leg didn't feel so bad, but his head was pounding. Why hadn't Natalie killed him? If she had hit his femoral artery, there would have been a lot of blood, and the wound to his head would have kept him unconscious for a while. It was almost like she had wanted to make it look like she meant to kill him.

"Can you take a deep breath for me?"

He did his best to comply.

"Good. You just have to get plenty of rest, drink lots of fluids, and eat what you can. Small amounts at first, okay?"

Nick nodded. "When can we take these out?" He lifted his wrist up to display the IVs. He hated anything medical.

"When you're hydrated and eating enough. How's your pain level?"

"It's fine," he lied.

"Are you sure, Nick?" Melissa called from her chair in the corner. She probably suspected he was hiding the truth. She knew how he felt about medicine.

"I'm fine, Mel. Really." Trying another painful smile, he turned to the nurse. "Is it okay if she sits next to me?"

"Yes, of course. But don't stay up for too long. You need to rest if you want to recover quickly, whether you want to or not."

"You're right to suspect that he's not a very good patient." Melissa dragged a chair over.

"I'll be fine. I've been through worse."

"I haven't." Melissa's face was wan, and she had dark circles under her eyes. "I was petrified I was going to lose you, Nick. And I'm so worried about Sidney, too." She pushed back the hair from his bandaged forehead. "I know why you kept looking for him." She kissed him on a small patch of uncovered skin on his brow.

"I promise I'll find Sidney for you. And, stop the NIH from running their despicable program."

Melissa clutched his hand. "Look at you. You're not going anywhere. Not for a while. Besides, Natalie said she could help me."

Nick started to lurch up, but the burst of pain in his head forced him back down. "Natalie? What do you know about Natalie?"

"She's here, Nick. She—"

Nick gripped the sheets. "What do you mean she's here? What the hell are you talking about?"

"She's in the other room."

His whole body tightened. "Send her in here right now. I have a few things to ask her."

"Nick, calm down. Sonya said—"

"Forget, Sonya. I'll rest after I've talked to Natalie." His anger darted toward Melissa. He didn't mean to direct it at her, but he couldn't understand why she would cooperate with that woman. It was frustrating as hell.

"Okay, I'll get her. But promise you'll listen to what she has to say. She was trying to help, Nick. When you hear her side of the story—"

He gritted his teeth. "Melissa, stop it. Just get her. I don't have the energy to talk about it."

Natalie stepped into the room. She had him at a disadvantage because she was well and standing, while he was weak and bedridden. His features tightened even more. The tension made his headache worse, and he grimaced.

Natalie swallowed. "Hi, Nick."

"Why didn't you kill me?"

"I see you're getting right to the point. Direct as always."

"Just tell me."

"I was ordered to. You're right about that, but just because the US government wants you dead it doesn't mean I do." Natalie took a step closer to him.

"Keep your distance. And, here's a different question. Why were you sent to kill me?"

She stood perfectly still as she answered, "I don't know. Nicholas, you know that most of the time they don't even tell us."

"I don't buy that. We've always been able to read between the lines."

Melissa intervened. "Nick, just let her explain."

Sighing, he turned back to Natalie. "Go ahead."

"My guess is you must have been getting too close to discovering the connection between CIRAS and Sunshine."

"What *is* the connection?"

"Honestly, Nick, I don't know. If I did, I would tell you."

"Why? You're an evil person."

Melissa interrupted, "Just hear her out."

Natalie told Nick the same story she'd told Melissa.

"Why didn't you just tell me the truth?"

"I was afraid they'd kill you first."

"That wasn't your decision to make."

She looked him in the eyes. "I know you're right. I'm sorry, Nicholas. Forgive me?"

Nick could see Melissa's entreating expression from the corner of his eye. Melissa had a soft heart, even though she didn't always show it. If she could accept all this from his ex-girlfriend, then shouldn't he be able to? Or he could at least try to put on a good show for her sake. She already had enough to worry about.

Natalie may have just been doing what she thought was right at the time. She had never understood that his honor was an essential part of who he was. By taking that away from him, she had injured him in her own way, even though she thought she was protecting him. But Melissa would never do that. She understood that quality in him. He would try to forgive Natalie for her sake.

"Sure. Fine," he said finally.

Natalie's eyes widened, as though she was surprised by his words. "Thanks."

"Tell me everything you know about Sunshine and CIRAS. Even if it doesn't seem significant."

Melissa got up and came to the side of his bed. "No Nick, not now. I can see you need rest."

"It can't wait."

"You look awful. You have to take a break."

He felt awful, too. "Fine."

"I can come tomorrow," Natalie suggested. "Nick, the CIA confiscated your phone, so we'll have to communicate through Melissa's."

CHAPTER 26

UNCIVIL SERVANTS

Nick surveyed the living room of the safe house from his perch on the sofa, finally free from the hospital bed. After another day hooked up to the IVs, he finally convinced Sonya he could do without them. No way was he at 100 percent, but he recovered quickly and wasn't worried about it.

Melissa slipped next to him, and he reached an arm around her. "How are you doing?"

She smiled crookedly. "You're the one who almost died, and you ask me how I'm doing?"

"I didn't almost die."

She raised an eyebrow, and Nick kissed her there.

Pulling away, she blurted, "I want to visit the Walkers. I know you went there, and—"

"No, Melissa. You have to stay here. You aren't safe out there—at least, not yet. Not until I know more. We can't chance it."

"You let Victoria leave."

"Melissa, look at me."

"What! I can't stop thinking about Sidney. Maybe the Walkers know something."

He hated seeing her in so much pain, but she couldn't leave. "They already told me everything they know. I won't have you put yourself at risk."

Her lips quivered as her eyes watered with tears. "But I hoped they could describe him to me, tell me something about him. I only had him for two weeks, Nick. I don't know anything about him." She wrinkled up her nose and sniffed.

"Come here." He held out his arms. She started to move into his embrace, but the doorbell interrupted them.

"That must be Natalie." Melissa sprung up and rubbed the tears from her eyes on her way to the door. I want to be here when you two talk."

"Okay."

Melissa opened the door, and Natalie walked into the living room. "I can't stay for long," she said as she started to take off her coat.

"Let me take that." Melissa took her coat and hung it on a hook by the door.

"Thanks. How are you feeling, Nick?"

"You said you don't have long. That means no time for small talk."

Natalie's eyes flashed with hurt but she nodded, looking around for a place to sit and settling on an armchair situated catty-corner from the sofa.

Melissa sat on the sofa near Nick. He could tell she was nervous by the way she fidgeted.

Natalie took a deep breath. "Okay, so here is what I know for sure. Like I said, I'm not assigned to the project, so I don't have full clearance. But I know that the NIH somehow sends the missing children from Sunshine to CIRAS, which the NIH funds.

"I think it's a safe assumption that the children become the Tabula Rasa think tank. Rumors are that no one has ever met a member of that group, so CIRAS is most likely hiding something about them.

"Considering how Sebastian Warner works and Dr. Maxwell's reputation, God only knows how they've been manipulated to be the human supercomputers everyone says they are. I have to admit I don't like the ideas my imagination comes up with. Hopefully, they aren't as bad as that."

Melissa looked stricken. "Wait a minute. Isn't Warner the guy Nick told me about? The one who authorized horrible experiments on prisoners? And Dr. Maxwell, what's his reputation?"

Before Nick could stop her, Natalie answered. "Yes, Warner is who you think he is. He isn't exactly known for his high moral standards."

Melissa interrupted. "So, the director of the NIH set up CIRAS? He designed experiments for Sidney and other children like him?"

Nick interjected, "Hey, we don't know any of that. Why don't you let Natalie finish telling us the things she's sure of?"

Natalie continued, "As far as I know, the NIH simply funds CIRAS. They didn't create it. But Warner probably knows what they're doing with those funds, and he's been known to accept bribes to sanction specific programs."

"Jesus," Melissa said, sinking into the sofa.

Natalie continued. "The center was founded by Randolph Jameson based on his seminal work on the nature of human genius. But Scott Maxwell took over everything years ago. And to answer your earlier question,

Melissa, Maxwell is reputed to be ruthless and to have even lower moral standards than Warner."

"We need to get Sidney out of there, Nick," begged Melissa.

"That's the plan. How much can you help us, Natalie?"

"Unfortunately, not much. And I can't come back here. I don't want to arouse anyone's suspicions. They're already starting to look for you, Nick. They haven't figured out how you got out of the hospital, but they're working on it."

"Can you give me weapons, devices, maps of CIRAS, anything?"

"There's a storeroom in the basement here. I'll give you the security code. Do you have something I can write on?"

Melissa jumped up. "I'll get a notebook."

"You'll find all you need there except the CIRAS maps," Natalie continued. "Sorry, I don't have access to those. And there is a computer with Wi-Fi in the office. The password is ricard1018."

Nick smirked. Her last name and birthday. Not very safe, but he chose not to comment.

Melissa handed Natalie a notebook and pen. She jotted down the code, ripped the page out, and handed it to Nick.

Nick reached forward to grab it and grimaced from the shooting pain that ran along his right thigh. "Thanks." He folded the paper and put it in his pocket. "How long can we stay here?"

"You're good for now. I'll text Melissa if you need to leave. Sorry, I can't help more. If I think of anything else, I'll send you a message. What about Sonya? Is she here? Do you need her anymore?"

Nick said, "No, I sent her home."

Melissa glanced at him sharply. "You said she had to run some errands and would be back."

He tried to give her what he hoped was a winning smile. "I'll be fine. You're the only nurse I need."

Ignoring his grin, Melissa replied, "I guess it's too late now."

Natalie rose from her seat. "I need to leave."

Melissa said, "I'll show you out."

"Natalie," Nick called out. She spun around. "Thank you." Nodding, her eyes softened and she walked out the door.

Melissa came back and sat down next to Nick. "How soon can you get Sidney out of there?"

"I'm not sure…"

Nick watched as Melissa's fear turned into panic. "Why aren't you sure?"

He tried to calm her down. "I need more information first. I may get only one chance, and I want to do it right."

Melissa twisted her hands in her lap. "Don't you know someone else from the CIA? Somebody like Natalie, but who can get you into CIRAS?"

"It's not that easy. We're lucky she was able to help us. The CIA is a complicated place with complicated people. If I went to the wrong person for help, it could get us killed." He shifted his body. His head was starting to ache. Though he hated to admit it, he felt like he should lie down. "Melissa, can we talk about this more tomorrow?"

Her face was no longer pale. Now it was bright red with frustration. "Tomorrow? Why can't you call one of your old CIA friends today?"

Nick snapped. "Look, Melissa—for one, I don't know how many people in the CIA know about the situation at CIRAS. Second, it's impossible to tell who can be trusted. Impossible! Do you get that?" He stopped and stared at her, hoping the information would sink in. His mouth twitched as he waited, but then he went on. "I don't know who might help us even if I knew I could trust them, which would be doubtful to say the least."

Melissa looked back at him, stunned into stillness by his backlash. He hardly ever got angry with her. But his head hurt, and he was tired, and he was, after all, human. "Melissa, I'm sorry. I'll find him."

Her expression softened. "I'm sorry too. I'm just so worried. I know you'll do everything you can."

Though Sidney was Melissa's sole focus, the program needed to be completely shut down and that would take time. But he couldn't tell Melissa that right now. She was a scared mother whose concern for her child had hijacked her perspective. "I'll figure it out, sweetheart." He tried to show his determination by looking into her eyes.

Tears tore out of her with gushing strength. Nick held her closer and wrapped his other arm around her so he could enclose her completely. "I'll get Sidney out of there."

Melissa's body trembled, and her breathing was irregular. She gulped pathetically for breath.

Nick held her tighter still and whispered in her ear, "I promise."

Melissa seemed to lose the battle with her tears and started sobbing again. She cried so hard that she was barely able to draw a breath. Nick just let her cry. It was the best thing for her.

Finally, worn out, she leaned against his chest. Her head was satisfyingly heavy against him. He kissed the top of her hair, and her limbs softened. Unexpectedly, that small movement made him want her. Not sure if she was open to his desire or if it would help her at this moment, he stroked her hair as he often did to let her know what was on his mind.

To his pleasure, she lifted her head and asked, "Do you want to go upstairs to one of the bedrooms?"

"I would like that very much. But you'll have to be gentle with me—nurse's orders." He grinned.

Melissa tried to smile. "What am I going to do with you?"

"I have a few good ideas."

CHAPTER 27

MANIC MAXWELL

When Jack finished his run, the pink and orange tones of the sunset undulated peacefully across the sky. A harsh thought cut through the beauty—the other residents were all cowards. Together they could create a strong force against Maxwell, but not one of them had returned his calls, even when he'd explained it was urgent. Elvis hadn't responded either, which was strange. He seemed like someone who cared.

Jack gazed at the fragmented shades of dusk reflected in CIRAS's glass exterior. Sweat dripped down his neck and was immediately chilled by the air, like a hand of ice grabbing him. The creepy feeling matched his growing anxiety. Nobody willing to stand up for what was right. Ellen. Ellen was. And that made him so afraid for her.

He closed his eyes, pulling both hands through his damp hair as he approached the building. He remembered his first day here and how beautiful and impressive the building had looked. Now he watched as if in a dream while the blue lasers confirmed his identity. The doors opened so silently, he felt he was being lured into a trap. Brushing aside the warning, he stepped inside. The sudden heat on his skin made his flesh tingle. He headed toward his apartment for a shower.

"Dr. Kerwin, did you have a nice run?"

Jack spun around. Maxwell. Jack hadn't seen him since the day he'd gone to his office. Deciding to play it cool, he said, "Yeah, it was fine," speeding up.

The Director jogged beside him. Jack didn't look his way. "Ellen's good in the sack, isn't she?"

Before his head knew what his hand was doing, he punched Maxwell across the jaw.

Maxwell fell back onto the tile floor with a disturbingly loud crack, his expression a mix of shock and anger. He looked around, bewildered. Had he never been punched before? That would surprise Jack. A lot of people must have wanted to. *I highly recommend it*, he thought.

The cruel man sat on his ass, fuming. Then he made a big drama over pressing a button on his watch as he glared at Jack. In no less than thirty seconds, CIRAS security guards stepped out of the walls. "Put him in cuffs and take him to my office."

Jack curled his hands into fists. "What? No!" He scanned the hall for a way to escape, but in every direction was a security guard coming toward him. Jack could run, and he could fight. But he couldn't take down eight security guards at once. He met Maxwell's dark, beady eyes. "You won't get away with this."

"I already have."

They cuffed him then pushed and pulled Jack through the hallways as Maxwell hurried in front. Jack didn't exactly resist, but he didn't make it easy for them, either. He twisted and kicked liberally, hoping to administer some painful bruises, if nothing else.

CIRAS's Director opened the door to his office, and the guards hauled Jack inside. "You can put him there." He pointed to a chair in front of his desk as he sat in his own. "Wait outside the door until I tell you it's okay to leave."

"Yes, Dr. Maxwell," they replied in unison, pushing Jack into the chair.

Jack shifted his position so his hands weren't pressing into his back. "What do you want with me?" He tightened his muscles, his body a spring ready to release.

Maxwell ran his tongue along his teeth in an unnerving way. "Why did you punch me, Jack? I only stated the truth."

Jack bit the insides of his cheeks to keep his mouth shut. He wasn't going to give Maxwell an additional excuse to lock him up or send him to the same psychiatric hospital as Jameson.

The man rolled his neck and sighed at the ceiling. "You know I sent her to you to distract you, don't you?" He brought his lazy glance back to Jack. "I own Ellen. She does nothing without my consent." Maxwell settled back in his chair as if the boast made him feel more relaxed and secure.

Jack's mind rejected Maxwell's words, but his stomach tightened. That was the original reason Ellen had come to him, but things had changed for both of them since then. Anxiety coiled in his muscles, and doubt pressed its way into his mind. The tension in his stomach unleashed, and in another impulsive move, he spat in the direction of Maxwell's highly polished shoes. It was childish, but he wasn't in the best frame of mind.

Maxwell sat up and looked at the gob of spittle that had just missed his right shoe. "I should kill you for that." It was an observation not a threat.

Jack flew up out of the chair. He needed to get out of here—now.

Maxwell rolled his eyes. "You're smarter than that, Jack. The guards are right outside." He flapped his hand in a downward motion as if giving a command to a dog. "Sit."

Jack didn't move but only because he didn't know what to do. His life hadn't prepared him for this moment. He thought. His wrists were tied, his ankles weren't. He balanced on the balls of his feet, poised to deliver a swift kick.

Maxwell frowned. "Tsk-tsk. You really should listen. Sit. Down." As he spoke, he opened the right drawer of his desk.

Jack bent his knees to gain better power.

"That's enough, Jack!" Maxwell pulled a revolver from the drawer and aimed. Jack froze. Maxwell's actions were calm, as if this were a daily activity for him, like brushing his teeth. He waved the gun at Jack carelessly. Was the safety off? Jack was sure it wouldn't disturb him if it accidentally fired.

Maxwell's face reddened, and he stood up, clutching the gun tighter. He walked around the desk. "Sit. Back. Down. Now. Or I shoot."

His brain considered and rejected options at a frantic pace. He sat.

Maxwell leaned his rear against the desk. He put a finger to his lips as he held the gun on Jack. "Hmm, now where was I? Oh yes, I was going to review all the times I sent Ellen to you." He tapped his lip. "The first time was after your fuss about the agreement, and then after you had the silly notion to go talk to Jameson. Then, of course, there was the last time."

"I came to her," Jack erupted, his control cracking. He was absolutely certain that Ellen hadn't known he was coming to her apartment that night.

Maxwell scratched his head and nodded slowly. "Hmmm, you're right on that one. My mistake, I guess that was a freebie. But it was still fun to watch."

Jack lunged.

Scott cocked the gun. "Down, Jack."

He froze.

"I'm in control here. It would be wise for you not to forget that. You and that other stupid resident..."

Which resident? *Jack wondered.*

"I have the backing of the CIA, the FBI, and the NIH. And, hmmm, whom have I forgotten? Oh, yes, the President." Maxwell smacked his lips. "The President of the United States is on my side, Jack, not yours." He offered a satisfied smile and nodded. "He knows how TR members are produced. And you know what? He doesn't mind one bit. He just wants us to keep up with the good work, pump out the new discoveries." Maxwell lifted the corners of his mouth in a terrifying leer.

Jack brought his gaze to his feet and thought hard. He had known it was bad here, but he hadn't realized how far the corruption went or how disturbed Maxwell was.

Maxwell rapped his gun on Jack's chair. "Pay attention to me."

Jack kept his eyes on the floor.

"Look at me!"

Jack kept defiantly still. Maxwell put the muzzle of the gun under his chin and forced his head up. "That's better."

Jack was acutely aware of the circle of pressure below his jaw, but he kept his expression blank. Maxwell brought his other hand to the revolver and pushed it deeper into Jack's skin until his head was forced back. His breath hissed onto Jack's neck. "Listen to me closely. I'm going to let you go, but if you make a single wrong move, I will kill you. I'll kill you, and no one is going to care."

Jack didn't respond.

"Oh, and there's something else you should know. Ellen loves me. She always has." His eyes had a manic look to them.

151

That made no sense. It was just more proof that Maxwell was delu-
sional. Why the hell did he need to believe Ellen loved him? That was
really messed up. If he was letting Jack go, it was because he couldn't
afford to get caught with Jack's murder on his hands, regardless of what
he said. So, there were some limits to what Maxwell could get away with.
Jack put away the thought for future reference and walked away.

CHAPTER 28

DANGEROUS DETERMINATION

J ack's knees quaked as he walked back to his apartment, his phone chiming. A text from Elvis. Finally. Good. But the words on the screen weren't.

> Jameson is dead.

Jack's stomach turned to lead and threatened to drop to his feet.

> What happened?

> They say it was suicide.

> Why don't I believe that?

> I don't believe it, either.

A few seconds elapsed then:

Don't do anything stupid.

Too late for that.

I'm serious. I've seen things I shouldn't have. This is a very scary place.

What are you talking about?

I can't explain. Just promise me you won't do anything dumb.

Tell me what you saw.

I can't.

Come on!

Too dangerous.

Jack stared at the screen, silently begging.

Elvis didn't text back. Jack jammed his phone into his pocket and walked faster. He had a bad feeling about Ellen's plan. Should he go to the police? The thought was desperate and irrational. They couldn't be trusted.

He needed to talk to Ellen.

Meet me in the courtyard now.

After several tense minutes, she responded:

OK see you in 5.

Ellen called to him, "Jack!"

Jack turned around, and despite the worry and doubt that burned in his stomach, he caught his breath when he saw her. "Hi, Ellen," he managed, approaching her and kissing her chastely on the cheek. They walked along a path that wove through small trees and bushes while he told her about what happened in Maxwell's office. "So you see now why we shouldn't go through with it."

Ellen stopped short, and Jack nearly fell into her. She swiveled her head sharply in his direction. "Jack, can't you see it's even more important now that I do? Scott has to be stopped, or he'll hurt someone else. Besides, I thought we had already decided."

Jack struggled to remain calm. "It will put you in too much danger."

Her eyes turned to steel. "I know the risks, Jack. They're mine to take."

"They murdered Jameson."

"I heard it was suicide."

"You don't actually believe that." He held her by both shoulders. "Do you?"

Ellen glanced around. "I need to sit."

Jack saw a bench across the way. "Over there." He led her by the elbow and guided her onto the seat. Putting an arm around her, she grasped the ends of his fingertips.

"I know it's dangerous. But I have to do it. I need to be the person I choose to be instead of the one I became by default." She looked at him. "Does that make sense?"

Yes, it did make sense. But he wished it didn't.

"Jack?"

"Yes. It makes sense. But I still don't want you to do it."

"I've been living selfishly for far too long. Those children..." Her expression became distant.

Jack didn't press. He held her tighter. As his arm arced around her, he felt the electricity run through it. He couldn't help but wonder what things might have been like for them if they had met at a different time.

"I can't sit anymore. Let's go over the plan again."

"Okay." Jack rose and reached out a hand to help her up. Ellen stood and walked beside him. Occasionally, she bumped into his shoulder or hip. The slight contact made his concentration scatter. He moved farther away from her, trying to keep his mind clear. He needed to focus on their plan to make sure they had it all straight.

"So Maxwell will be unconscious for a while. You sure the stuff will work?"

Ellen didn't say anything.

"Ellen, are you sure it will work?"

"Yes, I've used it before."

"You—?" Jack started to ask, but Ellen stopped him with a hand on his arm.

"Please don't ask."

Jack blew out the air that was in his lungs. "Yeah, sure."

"I'll tell you about it if you want, but it was a while ago, and honestly, it isn't really important. I just don't have the energy to explain. But I can if you need me to." She looked into his eyes, and he could tell that she meant it. There would be no more running from the truth for Ellen. Some part of him was proud of her, while the rest was petrified for her safety.

Still, Jack contemplated for a moment, evaluating her offer. He did want to learn more about her and her past, but he didn't feel like wasting time explaining things that didn't matter anymore, either. He understood her point. "It's okay. I trust you. Let's just move on."

Ellen blinked. "How can you trust me? You know Scott sent me to you those first couple of times. Scott told you."

"And you told me you were doing your job."

"Only at first. Then you started making me feel things and want things that I had forgotten about..." She paused and bit her lip. She looked up at him with no guile in her beautiful green eyes. "Or didn't believe I could ever have." She seemed more naked than she ever had, even with all her clothes off.

Jack reached for her hand and held it. "Like I said, let's move on."

"Okay, if you're sure?"

Jack had decided on his way back from Maxwell's office that he wasn't going to worry about why Ellen had come to him because he believed that she had changed. He believed in the best in her. "I'm sure."

Her eyes started to water. "Thanks, Jack. It means more than you can know." She kissed him quickly.

Jack's lips hungered for more of her, but he locked away his desire. As they continued to walk, he worked on being content with holding her hand. It felt right in his palm. Ellen looked so determined, intent on succeeding. Though he still wanted her, he couldn't help but admire her rare ability to change. He knew it was difficult to be able to see oneself honestly.

"So once he's unconscious," she said, "I'll text you and let you know. Then you can disable the monitoring systems like I explained and grab the list of security codes. After that, I can take you to the TR Center."

Their only option once they got to the TR Center would be to film everything they could and spread it on social media, then send that hard evidence to both local and national news stations. The governing idea was that once enough people knew the truth, it would be impossible for Maxwell or the government to keep a lid on it.

"Are you sure you want to go with me? I think Elvis might have seen some of it accidentally and it really spooked him."

"What did he see?"

Jack sighed. "He wouldn't tell me. He was too frightened."

Ellen stopped walking. "You see, that's why I have to do this."

Jack pulled her close to his chest. "I like the new Ellen. Bravery suits you."

She smiled slightly, and Jack swore he saw a shimmer of tears in her eyes. "Thank you, Jack." She tilted her face up to his, and Jack kissed her for a span that seemed untouched by time.

When he pulled away from the kiss and Ellen, he thought that with any luck, the plan would evolve with better precision after they began to implement it. He was aware that ideas and information had a way of flowing more smoothly once you had a direction to move in. They would both have to be ready to improvise.

As Ellen continued to talk, she drifted closer and closer to him. Each time she did, Jack made less of an effort to move his body from hers. He wasn't sure if she was doing it on purpose, and he wasn't sure if he cared. The end result was the same. Some part of his mind knew it could be the last time, and that threat of danger made him want her even more.

"So then ..." Ellen faltered.

"So then ..." Jack turned and made her body yield to his closeness. They were inches apart. He pulled her tight. "Back to my room?"

CHAPTER 29

THE LAST MISSION

Melissa peered over Nick's shoulder as he scrolled down the article on the founding of CIRAS. He stopped and they both reread the paragraph on the screen. An intriguing twist—turned out Maxwell was a trust fund baby. It fit. Wealth often enabled bad ideas as well as good ones.

Nick paged down a little more. He stopped at something even more interesting. Jameson had accepted Maxwell as a graduate student at Havard only after Maxwell's parents donated a new wing to the psychology center. The school probably forced Jameson to take him on.

On instinct, Nick switched the search to find images of CIRAS's director. The minute the first image appeared, he recognized the man right away, though he had never seen him before. He was short and bald, wore wire-rimmed glasses, and had small, dark eyes, just as Henry Walker had described him. The only thing Nick couldn't see in any of the pictures was his shoes, but he was sure they would be well polished.

"That's Dr. Maxwell?" Nick nodded. "I don't like the look in his eyes. He has an aura of malice around him." She shivered.

Nick saw the same thing, though he couldn't catalog it. Malevolence was stamped into Maxwell's features. Abruptly, he said, "Melissa, I need to go into the basement and have a look around." He left before she could answer, not wanting to waste time talking.

"I'm coming." She followed him.

As they descended the steps, Nick felt the weight of his task descend on him, too. He had forgotten what this kind of pressure was like, where the only option was success because peoples' lives depended on it. By leaving the CIA, he had left behind that kind of burden.

Melissa stood so close to him that he could feel the heat of her breath through his thin T-shirt. He punched Natalie's code into the security pad. The door sprung open, and he looked inside. It reminded him of old times.

The room had been outfitted well with all of the equipment he would need for his mission. As he contemplated the many different types of equipment on the shelves—password decoders, security scramblers, weapons—the walls started to feel too tight around him. He let his breath take away his resistance and plucked a Glock from the wall.

"Holy crap," said Melissa. "This is unbelievable."

Nick turned around.

She swallowed and looked at the gun in his hands.

"Welcome to the CIA."

Melissa nodded. "It looks like something out of a movie. Do you think you have what you need here to break into CIRAS and get Sidney out?"

Nick buried his sigh. He had to be honest with her. "Melissa, you realize that Sidney might not be at CIRAS, right? We don't know for sure he's one of the children they took. It might not be that straightforward."

Melissa stared at the weapons and devices on the wall for a moment before she turned to face him. "I know you're right." Her voice was soft.

"I will find him, wherever he is." He smoothed her hair back behind her ear. "But I still need to go into CIRAS no matter what. There are other children there, and we need to make sure they get out, too."

Melissa looked at him from underneath her lashes. "I know you do. I know this is about more than just saving Sidney. You're a good man, Nick. I'm lucky to have you." She said in a choked voice, "The world is lucky to have you."

"I'm lucky to have you, too." He kissed her forehead.

"I'm going back upstairs so you can work."

Nick smiled. She understood him. "Thanks."

He perused the contents of the room. Here in a ten-by-ten-foot space were all the devices he had used while he was still active in the CIA. There were also many new ones. He crossed his arms and wrinkled his forehead. Technology had come a long way in the past few years. He exhaled noisily. He had some work to do.

Even though he worked as a private investigator, it had been years since he had infiltrated a high-security building. Nick didn't doubt his ability to do it. The truth was he just didn't want to. Not really.

The CIA was inherently selfish and completely dominating. Working for them was like being in a relationship with somebody who was insanely possessive. For Nick to accomplish what he needed to at CIRAS, he would have to treat this job as if it were a CIA mission. He didn't want to turn on that cold, calculating side of himself, but it was the only way he could be single-minded enough to do what needed to be done.

When he returned upstairs, Melissa said, "I'm making some dinner for us."

He saw that the table was set and some candles were lit. It looked nice, but he wasn't in a state of mind to appreciate it. "Thanks," he said, knowing he sounded cold.

Melissa zigzagged through the kitchen, finishing up her preparations. "Can I get you some wine?"

"Is there any vodka?" He leaned against the counter not far from where she was working.

"I'll check." She found some and put the vodka, ice, and a splash of club soda into a glass. She handed it to him.

"Thanks." He took a deep swallow.

Melissa opened the oven and poked the potatoes with a fork. "Something on your mind?"

"No, I'm fine."

"Okay. Well, why don't you sit down? Dinner's just about done."

"Yeah, sure."

"Nick, what's up?"

"Nothing. What can I help with?"

Melissa sighed. "Nothing. Just go sit down. I'll bring dinner out in a minute."

"Okay." Nick took his glass and walked to the table.

Dinner was probably delicious, but he couldn't tell because he couldn't taste anything.

"Nick, I don't want to stay here anymore. I want to go home."

His head jolted up. He hadn't realized he was staring at his plate. "Melissa, that is out of the question."

"Who says?"

"I say." He didn't have time for this. He had too much to concentrate on. She didn't understand. "Melissa, don't do this."

"Do what?"

"Be impatient. Difficult."

She crumbled her napkin and held it in her fist. "You're the one being difficult!"

Nick held his tongue.

"You're being cold and distant. And you know how frightened I am! I need you now, Nick."

He closed his eyes. "I'm doing what I can. I just need to give my attention to my mission. I thought you got that."

"I do." She cast her eyes downward. "I don't." She glanced up again. "I don't know what to think. I'm confused and scared. I feel alone."

"You aren't alone!" His words shot out.

"Don't get mad at me."

Damn. His resources were low for handling this sort of thing. Finally, he managed to say, "I'm not mad at you."

"Then let me visit the Walkers."

Nick stood up, propelled by his frustration. "One has nothing to do with the other! It's not a punishment to keep you here. It's for your safety, Melissa. You have absolutely no idea what we're dealing with. The CIA, the Mafia, the NIH, and God knows who else are all in this together. That means there is no one, and I mean no one, we can trust for sure."

Melissa threw down the balled-up napkin like it was a gauntlet. She hadn't listened to anything he had said.

Nick watched it land on the table. He begged, "Please, Melissa, just trust me."

"I'm trying to. It's not easy. I'm going upstairs to lie down."

Nick let her go. It would be better if they were apart for a little while. He went back down to the basement to get reacquainted with his equipment.

CHAPTER 30

SEPARATE WAYS

D aylight slipped through the cracks between the wooden blinds, creating jagged lines of light and dark across the comforter and Melissa's body. Nick kissed her exposed shoulder, snatched some clothes off the chair in the corner, sneaking out of the room.

He placed his steps carefully until he reached the kitchen, not wanting to wake Melissa. He changed into the dark jeans, T-shirt, and leather jacket from upstairs, downed a cup of coffee and a stale donut and went into the office. He typed *ricard1018* into the keyboard and punched *CIRAS Center* into the search engine. He clicked on images and scrolled through, looking for a map.

In one photo he saw two posts in front of the main entrance. Those were probably screening devices, something to avoid. There would be more, but the security scramblers would take care of them. In a weird way, it was good that the US government had built CIRAS because their security systems would be familiar.

Nick used Melissa's phone to send a text to Natalie:

> Any chance you can get me an untraceable car?
> Need to run reconnaissance of CIRAS.

He waited for several minutes, but there was no response.

Still no sound from upstairs. Good, because he had to leave before Melissa was up. He found a few more images that might help him, printed them out, and stuffed them into a bag he found in the room. Then he went back to the basement.

He chose a Glock 27 subcompact .40 caliber off the wall, standard CIA issue. Then, he grabbed a tiny camera with long-range zoom capability and a recording device. He pushed them all through the opening of the black bag.

Melissa's phone vibrated in his pocket, and he looked at Natalie's response:

> Give me twenty minutes.

He sat down on the floor to wait. He wouldn't have to worry about making too much noise if he stayed down here until Natalie texted back. Mentally, he went over the functions of the new equipment. It had taken hours to familiarize himself.

The phone vibrated again.

> Go out the front door. Two blocks to your right, then one up to the left. Colonial Parking. Third floor. Facing Street. White Ford Explorer. Texas plates. Keys under back left wheel. Last time I can help. Good luck and be careful.

He sent a text thanking her, then closed the door to the storeroom and crept upstairs. When he got back to the first floor, he paused to listen. He couldn't hear anything. Melissa must still be asleep. He left her a note on the counter, anchored it with her phone, and slipped out the door.

The unseasonably cold November air hit Nick. It had been weeks since he had felt any fresh air on his skin. His face crinkled with a strange mix of pain and pleasure. His leather coat was too thin to keep him warm, but he chose not to think about it. Mind had to control matter. Life burned through him, and it was electrifying. This was the other side of a mission—the adrenaline, the excitement, and, he reluctantly admitted, the fun. He was surprised to find that he had forgotten this part.

Two blocks flashed by in seconds as he strode down the sidewalk. His concentration sharpened, and the present was all that existed. *One block to the left. Colonial Parking. Elevator to the third floor. Row facing the street. Ford Explorer. There.* He grabbed the key, put it in the ignition, and drove.

The rules were simple: One step at a time. Center on each one. Don't move on to the next until the previous is achieved.

His right thigh objected when he pressed down on the gas pedal, temporarily bringing him out of the "zone." Pain coursed down to his foot, but it wasn't enough to stop him. He drove unimpeded by the pain or anything else until he reached the outskirts of the CIRAS complex. He got himself back into that place of total awareness of the present, and everything slowed down.

Put the car in park. Take the black bag. Lock the car. Throw the keys in the bag. Get close to the building, but not too close. Avoid security cameras. Leave no trace.

Somewhere deep in his mind, Nick noticed the building's exterior. There was something sinuous and interesting about it. It looked better in person than it had on the Internet. But none of that was important.

Walk the perimeter. Take photos. Determine location of think tank. Check for exits and likely security points, vulnerabilities.

Nick's senses took in every detail. Smooth walls of glass and metal. Large doors, probably electronic. Scanning posts. Nobody outside. Nobody goes outside, maybe. Tabula Rasa must be in basement. Windows everywhere else.

How many were in there? He counted the windows, estimated the offices, extrapolated the number of people. Four residents. Where did they live? Where would he put them if he didn't want them to see anything?

Take pictures from all angles. Zoom in more. Go around the entire building. He froze as he heard a sound and turned to see someone jogging nearby. Get out of here, now! Before he sees you.

As Nick drove back, the pain in his leg was more challenging to ignore. It kept poking at him, demanding attention. His head didn't hurt much, though. He focused on that. After a couple more miles of driving, his single-mindedness dispersed, and he started to think about what Melissa would say to him when he got back. That did make his head hurt, so he tried to stop.

Colonial Garage was just around the corner. It felt like he had left there days ago, but it was only eleven a.m. He secured the car close to its original spot and headed back to the townhouse. Nobody followed him. Apparently, they hadn't figured out his location yet. There was no way to know how much time he had. He would have to infiltrate CIRAS soon, whether he felt ready or not.

Nick didn't bother to open the door quietly. Melissa was surely up already, and he couldn't hide from her once he was inside. He called out, "Melissa?"

Nothing. He immediately ascended the stairs and went into the bedroom, but she wasn't there, either. The hairs on the back of his neck arranged themselves in parallel lines, telling him what he already suspected. She wasn't here.

Nick raced down the steps and into the kitchen to look for Melissa's phone. It was gone, but there was a note in its place. He picked it up to read, but the print was too small. Damn it! Where were they? By the computer—he must have left them by the computer.

Nick went to the office, snatched his glasses from the desk, and shoved them onto his face. He threw himself into the chair and read the note.

Dear Nick,

I know you didn't want me to, but I needed to go talk to the Walkers. I want to find out more about Sidney. I know you'll worry, so I brought one of the smaller guns from the storeroom to protect myself. I've also placed a tracking device in my shoe so you'll know where I am. The monitor is in the office.

I'm sorry, Nick. Don't be upset with me. Try to understand that I had to do this.

I love you,

Melissa

Nick took off his glasses and threw them on the desk. They skidded onto the floor, but he didn't pick them up. Melissa had no idea what kind of danger she was in. Why hadn't she listened to him? He swiveled around and saw the monitoring device on the shelf behind him. He stared at it for a second, pocketed it, and headed back out the door.

CHAPTER 31

PAINTED WARRIOR

J ack roamed his apartment, searching for something to replace his feeling of helplessness. As he passed the office, he couldn't help but think of all the progress TR had made. Despite everything that was going on, he was still interested in the research, and that made him feel like an awful person. Was he just another selfish scientist?

Thoughts nagged and grew more difficult to ignore the harder he tried. So, he stopped trying. Maneuvering his shoulders through the entrance to the office, he sat down. As long as the work had already been done, there was no reason not to use it. It would almost be wasteful. It was only an excuse, and it made him feel guilty. But wasn't there some truth in it? He pulled a notebook and pen out of a briefcase that had been lying around.

Power up. Jack commanded. The screens to his right and left popped on. He positioned himself in front of the TR tablet to see the equations. *Jesus, looks like they've nearly figured it out already.* He scrambled to uncap his pen and flew to an open page in his notebook, almost tearing it. Like an electrocardiogram machine, he scribbled down information at a frenetic speed.

He spent several hours copying all the important information, not taking a break except to get some water and use the bathroom. Half the time he was thrilled by what TR had figured out, and the other half he couldn't help but wonder what had been done to them to make them so brilliant.

The uncomfortable truth was that Jameson and Maxwell had been right. Whatever they had done here, however immoral, illegal, or cruel, it had worked. TR was the most successful computer in the world—except it wasn't powered by binary code and electronics. It was fueled by the sheer strength of unadulterated human genius. Jack found it incomprehensible that TR had achieved in a couple of months what he had struggled to do for years. And, it would all come to an end when he revealed CIRAS's cruelty to the world. That was the bitter reality.

Jack transcribed the most crucial information. There was too much to write down every line. Ellen would have to act when she saw the opportunity. Neither one of them knew exactly when that might be. It could be tonight, or it could be days from now. Either way, they had to be ready.

Jack thrust the notebook in a backpack and stuffed it under the bed. Then sat, his head in his hands, wondering what to do next.

The buzz of his phone startled him. Lifting his head up, he saw the message on the screen:

Going to Scott's tonight.

Now it begins. Blood pounded through his temples. He thought he could hear it echo in the room. He typed his reply:

Be careful.

Ellen sat at the vanity in her bathroom and applied her makeup. The heaviness of the moment intruded, and her hands moved reluctantly, as if through thick liquid.

It was difficult to get Scott to agree to see her. She always could read him well and knew he wasn't really interested in getting together. And yet, as usual, his weird attachment to her caused him to agree anyway. Though his reluctance would have consequences. She would have to allow him to demean her in bed. That never failed to turn him on when he was having trouble getting into it.

Ellen submerged her worries, dipping her brush into a sable-colored shadow. She held her eyelid taut with her index finger as she applied the hue in smooth, broad strokes. She repeated the process with the other eye, taking her time. She pulled her face back from the mirror to check the results, adding a bit more shadow to the crease of her right eye to match the other precisely.

She hadn't had sex with Scott since she had started things back up with Jack, and the thought of having to let him inside her flooded her stomach with acid. How had she managed to get herself so involved with such an unstable person? Why hadn't she seen the signs when she accepted his job offer?

Because he'd gotten her out of her mother's clutches. And, initially she hadn't seen how truly cruel he was. By the time she did, it was too late. Beating herself up wouldn't help anyone now. She concentrated on applying her eyeliner.

Putting on makeup calmed Ellen. Part of her was soothed by her ability to make herself look beautiful, it was a part she hated. She reminded herself she was doing something brave—brave and important. Something that would make her father, had he been alive, proud of her. She had a new angle from which to view herself and this evening. Her makeup became war paint, and the seductive clothing she put on would be her armor.

She was doing something tonight that she was not sure she had ever done before, standing up for what she believed in. She was surprised to find that it gave her strength that extended beyond the tenuous power of lipstick and high heels.

The ceremony complete, she spun her eyes to the full-length mirror in the corner, assessing her image with newfound disinterest. Her smooth, high bun emphasized her kohl-lined eyes and full lips. Turning her back to the mirror, she looked over her shoulder. The forest-green halter dress was high at the neck but came down low in the back. The hanging fabric just grazed the place where her back ended and her ass began. The front hem reached her knees, while the back fishtailed near her ankles, repeating the lines of its open back suggestively. She evaluated her dress like a scientist, with cool remove.

Ellen extended her wrist away from her body and looked down at it. The gold and snakeskin cuff on her right wrist matched her black snakeskin heels. The bracelet seemed like a shield. Its dramatic size emboldened her narrow wrist. She prayed for its protection tonight.

Jack knew he should stop Ellen. Tonight she was walking willingly into the lair of a monster. What the hell had they been thinking? Had they actually convinced themselves they could bring down CIRAS on their own? It had been stupid and ill-planned. Jack felt panicked. He wanted to run to Scott's apartment and pull Ellen out of there as soon as possible. He wanted to scream at her to forget the whole thing. *Jesus Christ, she could be killed!*

On top of that, Elvis had gone MIA, too. Jack hadn't seen or heard from him in days. He suspected that Elvis had pragmatically decided it was better to stay out of the way and keep his mouth shut, especially after what had happened to Jameson. Jack could describe the action as cowardly but really it was just practical.

Jack clamped his teeth together and unconsciously balled his hands into fists. Staying away—that was what he should have told Ellen to do, instead of supporting a plan that put her in real danger. Guilt made him ask himself if she was just trying to prove herself to him so he wouldn't judge her for her past.

CHAPTER 32

TRACKING

N ick turned the corner in the parking garage. The Ford was still there. He said a silent prayer of thanks to a god he didn't believe in. As he pulled the keys out from behind the wheel, he thought of Natalie. She was the one he owed a thank you—a genuine one.

He started the engine and looked down at the tracker, which showed Melissa was on her way to the Walkers'. He had to head her off. Revving the engine, he drove out of the garage faster than he should have.

Nick didn't refer back to the tracker. He knew the way, having a photographic memory for directions. One trip was enough to make an indelible imprint.

Before he was mentally ready for it, the small, white Cape entered his field of view. He parked in front. He got déjà vu—except it wasn't, not really. He had been here before. How could he ever forget? His memory pierced him like a sharpened knife. The image of Maxwell spun into his mind. The "uncle."

Before he left the car, he instinctively glanced at the tracker on the passenger seat. The dot had moved. Melissa wasn't here. Where had she gone now? As Nick looked through the windshield, he felt scared and angry in equal measure. *Melissa, why didn't you just listen and stay put?*

Nick had one eye on the road and the other on the moving blue circle. The dot's trajectory altered sharply. Nick careened into the right lane to keep pace with it and unintentionally cut off a green Subaru. The driver laid on his horn. The noise rattled in Nick' skull, intensifying his urgency. He had to reach her quickly. She was in too much danger out in D.C. alone. He couldn't protect her if she wasn't with him.

The dot sprinted ahead in a quick spurt. Nick lunged the Ford in front of another car, a Porsche. The Porsche driver wasn't inclined to blare his horn in complaint. Instead, he zipped to his left and wove his car around and directly in front of Nick's. The driver slowed down immediately, and Nick had to slam on the brakes to keep from smashing into him. *Asshole!*

Jiggering into the left lane, he pressed the accelerator as far down as it would go. He zigzagged through the lanes of traffic, his movement controlled by a cocktail of instinct and adrenaline. The Porsche driver didn't bother him again after his one road rage move had been exhausted. Nick couldn't even find the jerk in his rear-view mirror. He stopped maneuvering through traffic and slowed down. He checked the tracker. Melissa was farther ahead now and headed toward the Third Street Tunnel.

Speeding up, he entered the tunnel. Traffic was tight, and he couldn't tell which vehicle Melissa was in. He examined the possibilities as he drove closer to her. Soon the blue dot transformed into the car directly in front of him, a black Cadillac with heavily tinted windows. Nick's forehead tightened. Melissa didn't know anyone who owned a car like that. She couldn't have borrowed it, and she wouldn't have had time to rent it.

Nick swallowed. Someone had kidnapped her. It was the middle of the day, for Christ's sake. Whoever had taken Melissa was pretty damn ballsy or they just knew they would get away with it. He wasn't happy with either choice because both were signs of a professional.

He let up on the gas and allowed a few cars to fill up the space between him and the Cadillac. He followed the car at a distance until it pulled off at the next exit. Nick did, too. It took a sharp turn at the corner and into the back parking lot of a warehouse with a *For Lease* sign on the front. Nick drove past the building and parked a couple of blocks away. He took out the Glock, holding it low alongside his thigh.

He walked casually but quickly past the buildings on his right until he reached the one with the *For Lease* sign. He edged around to the side of the warehouse, his back inches away from the wall. When he reached the corner of the building, he glanced around to the back. The Cadillac was there, and one other car, a silver Mercedes.

A large man in dark clothing pushed Melissa ahead of him. She lurched forward, her hands bound and her mouth gagged. She didn't seem to be resisting, which was the right thing to do for now.

Someone opened a door for them from the inside, and the big man thrust Melissa before him into the warehouse. The door thudded shut behind. Nick clenched the Glock, waited a few minutes, and tried the door. The deadbolt was locked tight, and he didn't have his tools with him to open it. He slipped around to the front to try the door there.

This one had a simple lock. Nick scanned the vicinity to make sure no one was watching, and when he saw that it was clear, he rapped the butt of his gun on the lock to knock it open. After a couple of tries, it gave way. He glided inside, gun cocked.

The interior appeared to be a large storage room filled with stacked boxes. So far, he didn't see anyone. He drew in a lungful of air. They must all be in the back. Glock held next to his chest, Nick clung close to the wall as he turned the corner into the adjacent room. He could hear two male voices, but he wasn't close enough to figure out what they were saying. He followed the sound, being careful to stay hidden.

Nick darted toward the voices, ducking behind piles of boxes as he moved. Finally, he was close enough to hear clearly. He quieted his breathing and listened.

He knew that voice.

CHAPTER 33

BOWING TO CRUELTY

"Hold on, Ellen."

Ellen startled at Scott's voice, then silently cursed herself for her skittishness. She was being silly. Scott had obviously seen her on one of his monitors as she stood in the hallway in front of his apartment.

He opened the door just as she was bringing her face and body back to an expression and posture corresponding with the evening of seduction she'd planned for him.

Scott leered at her. "I surprised you?" It was less a question than an accusation.

"No, no, of course not." She smiled from beneath her darkened lashes. "I'm sorry."

Scott thrust out his chest. "Oh, don't worry. You'll make it up to me." He reached for her hand and yanked it hard, pulling her into the room with a strength she'd never felt from him. She had to shift her balance quickly to keep from tripping on her high heels. Biting her lip hard, she tasted lip gloss. Thankfully, no blood.

"Stand up straight, Ellen."

Ellen stood up, starting to smooth out her dress.

"Stay still."

She let her hands drop to her sides.

He walked behind her with purposeful strides and slammed the door shut as she stood firm, uncertain what game he was about to play. It scared her that he already had the upper hand. Often she was able to manipulate him while offering the semblance of control. So far tonight, it was Scott who was in charge.

He stalked back toward her. "I'm going to teach you a lesson tonight, Ellen." His eyes gleamed with excitement and vindictiveness.

Ellen felt like prey. Her mind grasped for a way to shift the power balance between them.

Scott shoved her on the shoulder. "Get on your knees."

Good, she knew what he wanted. Ellen nearly sighed with relief. This was predictable, at least. She instantly felt safer, reaching up to unzip his pants.

"No!" he slapped her hand away viciously. "You will do what I ask as I ask it and not before. I told you I need to teach you a lesson. You do nothing without my command."

Sometimes Scott liked to pretend he was the master and she the slave. Something was different this time, though. His tone had true brutishness in it. There was an edge to him that he hadn't shown her before. Maybe he had spied on her while she was with Jack in the courtyard and was jealous. Ellen had to redirect him. "Of course," she stated emphatically. She paused and added, "Master."

"That's right." Scott glowered. "I am your master. Now I want you to crawl on your knees until I tell you it's okay to stop." He put his hands on his hips and jerked his chin forward as a signal for her to crawl. Reluctantly she obeyed, crawling toward a corner of the room. Then she turned and crawled back toward him. Her movement was liquid and seductive over the unyielding surface. She gave him her best smoldering look with her heavily-lined eyes.

"Not like that. Go faster! And don't wave your ass so much! I will have you when and if I want to. I won't have you trying to convince me otherwise." He kicked her hard in the rear to emphasize his point. Ellen fell down brutally onto her elbows. She propped herself back up, afraid to disobey him.

She did as he asked, shortening her pace and moving with quick strides on her knees. The marble beneath them was cold and unyielding. Before long, they began to hurt. Her pride and self-preservation pulled at her, straining her emotions to their snapping point.

Her discomfort must have begun to show on her face, because Scott barked, "Oh, it hurts, does it? Well, go faster, then!" He hit her across her back, and it stung. She pressed her lips together tightly to hold back a scream. Scott was hurting her more than he ever had before. She was certain he knew about her and Jack. She had to appease him before he took this any further.

Ellen harnessed her fear and pain by concentrating on the patterns she made as she crawled. She traced large triangles across the surface, then moved to circles, then squares, then a star shape and back to triangles. Having something to focus on providing just enough of a distraction to give her the strength to continue.

When her knees hurt so much she was sure they would begin to bleed, she counted her steps in sets of twenty-five. As Ellen sustained her demeaning march about the room, Scott stopped watching. In her peripheral vision, she saw him sit down in a chair in the corner, pick up a nearby book, and flip through it in the most desultory manner. He didn't give her another glance.

Ellen thought about asking him if she could stop, but he might take that as an opportunity to hurt her more. What was he after? She scrambled for a way to sidetrack him. Maybe now would be a good time to try to get him sexually interested. He might be turned on after seeing her so humiliated.

Ellen wrinkled her brow. Something in Scott's manner suggested that wasn't what he was after. So what was it? She thought hard but couldn't find an answer.

Her body pulsed with pain. It was getting harder and harder to ignore. She looked over at Scott, her knees screaming for mercy. He had put the book on his lap face down and closed his eyes. Maybe he was becoming uninterested. Ellen took a chance and stopped crawling. She rested back on her haunches and lifted her knees off the marble.

Scott's voice thundered through her. "Who said you could stop? I'm not a fool. I may not be able to see you while my eyes are closed, but I can hear you. You are an idiot, Ellen. Move."

She brought one knee forward to meet the hard floor and squeezed her eyes tightly to keep from crying. She made several more patterns across the room until her knees simply would not allow her to continue to place one after another.

She looked down at them. Thin streams of blood trickled down her pale flesh and smeared the white marble with streaks of red. She couldn't tolerate the pain anymore. She decided to deal with whatever consequences came and stood up, gasping from the flash of pain that came from straightening her knees after they had been bent for so long. She ran her hand along her smooth hair and swallowed. "I'm leaving." Her voice sounded tired but clear.

Scott bounded from his chair, letting the book slide to the floor. "No. You. Are. Not. Ellen, get back down on your knees. I don't know why you came here, but you are not going to get what you wanted out of me. But rest assured, I will get what I desire out of you. And right now, I need you to kneel." He gritted his teeth as he spat out the words.

Staying resolute, she straightened her back and lengthened her neck, literally rising to his challenge. "I'm not playing your stupid little games anymore, Scott. I'm going." The hem of her dress swished around her ankles as she turned her back to him.

Ellen heard a drawer open, followed by odd rustling sounds, like something being unwrapped from cloth. Ellen hesitated momentarily, caught off guard. She didn't want to wait to find out what he had taken out of that drawer. She ran.

Scott's voice sounded like talons scraping through the air. "Turn around."

The menace in his tone forced her feet into a sprint. She took several desperate steps before his next words turned her legs to stone.

CHAPTER 34

ALIENS OR WORSE

Jack paced his apartment, resisting the urge to pour himself a drink, when he received a text from Elvis:

> Jack, can I come over? Need to talk.

In five minutes, Elvis was at his door. He looked bad. His hair was disheveled, and he seemed to have lost a lot of weight since Jack had last seen him. He'd already been thin to start with; now he looked like a skeleton. Perspiration speckled his forehead, and the edge of his collar was stained with sweat.

Jack peppered him with questions and comments. "Elvis, you look like hell. Come in. What are you doing here? Why the sudden change of mind to start talking to me again? Where the hell have you been?"

Elvis's head jerked back as if the questions amounted to a physical assault. "Um, can I sit down, please?"

Jesus, Jack, can't you see he's scared already? his conscience admonished. "Yeah, sorry. Sit anywhere."

Elvis chose an armchair in the sitting area by the window, and Jack joined him.

"So, why did you change your mind?"

Elvis shrugged in a jittery manner. It looked like he was being electrocuted. His eyes bulged more than normal. "I began to realize I shouldn't trust Maxwell to keep his word."

Jack brought his eyebrows close together. "His word about what, Elvis?"

"That he wouldn't kill me if I didn't say anything about what I saw."

Jack grasped the arms of his chair and leaned forward. "I think you'd better start from the beginning."

Elvis nodded. "Yeah, okay." He looked around skittishly. "Can I have a glass of water?"

Jack puffed out a breath. He pointed to the kitchen. "Over there. Help yourself." He watched as Elvis poured himself a glass of water. His hands trembled badly, and the drops of perspiration on his forehead had multiplied. He threw his head back and swallowed the water in one gulp as if it were a shot of tequila.

Compassion made Jack move to stand beside, placing a hand on his shoulder. "Hey, man, do you need something stronger?"

Elvis appeared grateful for the offer. "That might be a good idea. How about a gin and tonic?"

"Sure. I'll make us each one. You go sit back down, and I'll be there in a minute."

Jack prepared the drinks and carried them back to the sitting area. He handed one to Elvis, who immediately took a large sip. Jack seated himself and waited for Elvis to begin.

Elvis took another sip and followed it up with a loud sigh. He settled back in his chair and began his story. "About a week ago I couldn't sleep, so I decided to take a walk, you know?"

Jack nodded, impatient to hear the rest.

Elvis swallowed some more of his drink. "Well, I heard a noise down the hall, someone talking to himself, and I don't know what got into me, but I decided to see who it was. As it turned out, it was Maxwell. I could see him, but he hadn't seen me yet, and then I got another stupid idea. I started to follow him."

Jack raised his eyebrows. He wouldn't have expected that from Elvis. "What made you do that?"

Elvis shook his head. "I don't even really know. It was late, and like I said, I couldn't sleep. Part of the reason I couldn't sleep was because I kept thinking about Tabula Rasa—you know, wondering what they were like. Kind of a morbid curiosity, I guess. Plus, a little guilt—"

"So, anyway, you followed Maxwell."

Elvis nodded. "Yes, but at a distance. It wasn't that hard not to be noticed, because he was making a lot of noise. He walked with heavy steps and never stopped muttering to himself. The only time he was quiet was when he had to enter security codes to get through the doors."

Jack blinked in confusion. "Wait a minute. How did you get through the doors after him if you needed a code?"

Elvis finished his drink and placed the glass on the side table adjacent to his chair. "I was able to see a little bit. Plus, I listened. I have a talent for figuring out a code by sound. Anyway, the code was simple, just 1011. And they were all the same, too."

Jack pressed his lips together and thought. "That date seems familiar."

"Yeah, I don't know?" Elvis brushed aside Jack's comment and continued. "So I followed him through all these doors until we got close to the

Tabula Rasa center. And when he got there, I saw this tall guy in a suit waiting for him."

Jack slapped a hand to his forehead. "Hold on, I got it. That's the founding date of CIRAS, October 11. Not a very secure code. Sorry for interrupting. Go on."

Elvis wrung his hands together. "Mind if I get another drink first?"

"No, go ahead."

Elvis got up, and Jack contemplated the strange curve of the window to his right. It was convoluted, just like CIRAS. He turned away and sipped his gin and tonic.

It was good that Elvis had given him the security codes or, as it turned out, the security code. He and Ellen could skip the step of grabbing the list and go directly to the TR Center. It would save potentially crucial time.

Elvis collapsed back in his chair. He wasn't sweating as much now. Maybe talking had helped, or maybe it was the alcohol. Either way, he didn't seem as panicked.

"Who was the man in the suit?"

"I don't know. But they seemed to know each other well. Not friends exactly, but almost like business partners."

"What happened next?"

"Maxwell opened the door to the actual TR Center, and I caught a quick glimpse of the inside, and I freaked. I ran in the other direction and forgot to be quiet."

Jack unconsciously leaned forward. "What did you see?"

"Nothing too specific. Just creepy dark rooms with these pale, alien-looking figures inside. They definitely didn't look human. I panicked. I know I shouldn't have. It was stupid." Elvis's cheeks turned red with embarrassment.

"You didn't see anything else?"

"No, like I said, I panicked."

"Did Maxwell catch you after that?"

"Not right then, but the surveillance cameras had already caught me. The next morning, he called me to his office and told me that if I let anyone know what I had seen, he would kill me. He said it just like that as if it were no big deal." Elvis shifted his gaze to the window.

"I can believe that," Jack said, recalling his run-in with Maxwell. "Anything else?"

"Well, he also wanted to make sure I didn't tell anyone about the man who was with him."

That was a curious thing for Maxwell to demand. Jack commented, "But you said you didn't recognize him."

Elvis shrugged. "That didn't seem to matter." Elvis looked at his drink but apparently decided against taking another swig. He stared at Jack. "I want to help you end it. Those things, people, whatever they are—the TR group—it isn't right. They have to be freed, rescued...something..." His words trailed off.

Jack met Elvis's eyes. "Let me tell you what we have planned."

As soon as Elvis left, Jack's dread returned. It had been too long. He should have heard from Ellen by now. *Damn it.* Should he go to Maxwell's apartment, or would that put her in more danger? He slammed his palm against the wall, and the blow reverberated harmlessly through its surface.

It was difficult to decide what to do. Adrenaline pumped insistently through his blood and implored him to act. His strongest and most primitive impulse was to run to her. But maybe everything was going fine. Maybe she would be back here in a few hours, telling him that Scott was unconscious. Then they could continue with their plan. Or maybe, if she came back, he should just convince her and Elvis to leave this place with him.

Jack was used to being in control. Now feelings of doubt and hesitation invaded his brain like hallucinogens. Then something primal took over, annihilating thoughts and replacing them with movement he couldn't control.

CHAPTER 35

BEHIND ENEMY LINES

A nger coursed through Nick's bloodstream, as potent as any drug, but he refused to let it control him. Instead, he held completely still so he could listen as he crouched behind the stack of boxes.

Sebastian Warner said, "You can go, Mario. I got this."

"You sure, boss?"

"Yeah. Tell Alfonso thanks for taking care of the problem on such short notice. I'll send him double the normal amount."

"Will do, sir. Anything else?"

"That's all."

The back door of the warehouse slammed shut, and Warner spoke again. "So how long do you think it will take for your boyfriend to come rescue you? He's a resourceful fellow. My best guess is about three or four hours, tops. That gives us a lot of time together. How do you think we should spend it, Ms. Ryder?"

Nick recoiled at Warner's words. He wanted to run in there right now and rip Warner's head off, but he didn't. It wasn't the right time.

"What, no suggestions? Oh, that's right, you can't talk with that gag in your mouth. Let me take it off for you." Nick thought of Warner touching Melissa, and it was even more difficult to stay still.

"I have nothing to say to you."

"You should have told that boyfriend of yours to stop snooping around. Then we could have avoided all of this. It's really his fault, you know. He should have minded his own business."

Melissa screamed, "Shut up!" Nick was sure she knew her words were impotent, but he understood that sometimes you just needed to scream. Things got quiet for a little bit afterward, and that made Nick nervous because he couldn't see what was going on.

Finally, he heard Warner say, "Do you even know who I am?" There was silence as Warner waited for an answer. "Suddenly quiet, are we? You should be very interested me." Warner's voice got low and deadly. "I'm director of the NIH. Your son, Sidney, is part of my most important program. Unfortunately, he isn't responding well to his training. We may not be able to keep him for much longer."

"You asshole!" Nick heard the sounds of a chair scraping on the concrete floor. They must have tied Melissa to it, and now she was trying to reach Warner. Then he heard a loud clunk. The chair had fallen to the floor, he guessed. *Now!*

He ran into the room with his gun pointed at Warner. "Don't move!"

Warner squinted at him askance. "Oh, hi, Nick. Nice of you to join us. I do like threesomes. But you're earlier than expected." Warner started to raise the gun in his left hand, but Nick was quicker. He shot Warner twice in the upper left shoulder, and he collapsed backward.

Nick ran over to Warner, pulled the gun from his grasp, and slid it into a corner of the room. He called to Melissa, "Hang in there, Mel. I'll help you up in just a second. Got to take care of this asshole first."

"I wish you had killed him."

"You're messing with the wrong person, Nicholas Sperry," Warner said as he thrashed beneath Nick. "You have no idea what you've gotten yourself into."

"Want to enlighten me?" Nick growled. He secured his Glock in the waistband of his pants as he held Warner down with the weight of his body. He removed his own belt with one hand and used it to bind Warner's wrists together.

"You'll have to figure it out on your own," Warner snarled. "If you can."

As Nick leaned in to pull Warner's belt off his waist, Warner suddenly lurched up and knocked his forehead into Nick's. The blow forced him sideways. Moving with the speed of a viper, Warner grabbed Nick's gun and hopped up.

Melissa screamed, "Nick!"

Nick scrambled to his feet before Warner had time to aim and ran to get Warner's gun from the corner. He snatched it up as Warner fired the Glock. The shot just grazed Nick's forearm, nicking his flesh, but it was enough to make him drop the gun. It clattered to the floor.

As Nick reached down to pick it up, Warner said coolly, "I wouldn't do that if I were you."

Nick's hand hovered above the weapon. He looked over to see his Glock aimed at him, held up awkwardly between Warner's tied hands. Melissa was behind Warner, still on the floor, secured to the fallen chair.

Melissa swung her chair to hit Warner in the back of his calves. It wasn't enough to make him fall, but it caught him off guard. Nick jumped up and thrust a kick into Warner's abdomen. Warner crumpled beneath the blow. Nick stripped the Glock from his grasp and slammed Warner's head into the concrete wall. The blow knocked him unconscious.

Melissa sighed. "Thank god."

Nick looked at her, still toppled sideways. "Sorry, honey." He righted the chair and began to untie her.

"It's okay. Don't want the bad guy to get away, right? Nick, I'm so sorry." She pulled him close in a hug.

"What am I going to do with you, Melissa? You should listen to me."

She looked up at him with feigned innocence. "Maybe I've finally learned my lesson. I really am so sorry."

"I'm just glad you're okay." He leaned down and kissed her.

"Me, too."

Melissa regarded Warner's immobile body. "Shouldn't you tie him up more securely than that?"

Nick nodded. "Definitely."

He took off Warner's belt and used that to tie his ankles together. He unfastened the belt on Warner's wrists so he could secure them in back instead. Then he reached into Warner's pocket and pulled out a phone, which he slipped into his own pocket. Finally, he ripped off Warner's tie and used it as a gag. That would take care of him for now.

"What about your arm?" Melissa asked.

Nick stared at his forearm. "It's nothing."

"It's not nothing."

There would be no dissuading her. When they returned to the Explorer, she used some gauze and tape from the first aid kit in the glove box to patch Nick's wound.

When she was finished, Nick said, "Thanks."

"No problem. Now get in the passenger's seat. I'm driving."

Nick glanced at her.

"I'm driving," she repeated. "Give me the keys. You're injured."

"I'm not—"

Melissa reached out her hand. "Keys."

Nick sighed and pulled them out of his pocket. He placed them on her palm, and she closed her fingers around them. "Thanks."

She drove them back to the house without incident. "Why would Warner want you to come rescue me?"

"I think that's obvious. He was going to make sure I got killed for real this time. Warner said he was expecting me later, so he couldn't have realized you had a tracker on you. I'm sure if I had arrived when he expected, he would have had backup ready, and I might not have had a chance."

Melissa frowned. She looked skeptical. "But he's just the director of the NIH, not the CIA or FBI or any of that. How is he involved in the CIRAS cover-up, and why does he care?"

"Warner has always had his hands in a lot of pots. He likes money, a lot. As Natalie said, he isn't afraid to take bribes to push an unsavory agenda. My guess is that Mario and Alfonso are with the Mafia. Maybe I'm jumping to conclusions, but those sound like Mafia names if I've ever heard them. And we know Warner paid them to kidnap you. So, that's another clue."

Melissa looked out the windshield and tapped the steering wheel with her index finger. She seemed to be trying to put all the pieces together. "Do you think the Mafia was a go-between for Warner and the people who wanted to run illegal programs? Maybe CIRAS houses more than just the TR project. Maybe they have other experiments there that are hidden in the TR area or something. And those people are the Mafia's clients."

"Certainly, sounds plausible to me," Nick said as Melissa turned down the street where the safe house was located. He thought back to the prisoner manipulation project he had uncovered. It was all starting to become clear.

Melissa's phone vibrated in the drink holder between them. Nick picked it up and opened the message. "It's a message from Natalie: 'They found Warner. They will find you and arrest you soon. Make sure you aren't found. Go to CIRAS tonight. The evidence you get there will protect you.'"

Melissa blanched. "Oh crap, Nick!"

"It's fine. I'm ready, anyway."

"I have to come, too. If Sidney—"

Nick glared at her. "After what just happened? You can't be serious."

She appeared abashed. "You're right. But what am I going to do, wait at the house? That might not be safe, either."

Melissa pulled into Colonial Garage and drove up three levels before Nick finally responded. "I know, but I don't think the house has been identified yet, and it's a hell of a lot safer than taking you with me. I promise to come right back and tell you what happened."

Melissa shook slightly, and he could see that she was crying. He put a hand on her leg and squeezed.

She sniffed. "Okay," she whispered. "I trust you."

CHAPTER 36

UNDER THE GUN

E llen's gut told her running away was the more perilous option. She pivoted slowly. At another time, the sight of Scott holding a gun would have been laughable because he was so unmasculine, but now his eyes—small, pitch black, and furious—offered conflicting evidence. Ellen saw in their uncompromising blackness the truth about him. He would kill her, and worse than that, he wanted to. She wished she could believe he wouldn't do it, but then she would be lying to herself again. She wasn't going to do that anymore. Look where it had gotten her.

"I can explain about Jack."

"This isn't about Jack."

Ellen brought her brows together in confusion. *What?*

"You can screw him all you want, for all I care. I don't want you any-more." Scott took a threatening step toward her. "But—oops—hold on a second. I guess if I shoot this gun and kill you—" He waved it with a little swooping side-to-side motion, and Ellen briefly contemplated trying to grab it. But he straightened it upon her once again before she could make a decision. "You won't be able to do anyone at all, Ellen." He smiled with cruel pleasure. "Not ever again."

His high-pitched tone was too sweet. It gave Ellen chills.

"I told you I could explain."

Scott's face flushed with rage. "And I told you it's not about that. Why don't you ever listen to what I say? You believe me, Ellen, don't you?"

Ellen remained immobile. She flicked her eyes right and left, looking for a way out of this nightmare.

"You believe me, don't you?" Scott repeated. He took another step toward her, narrowing the distance between them. He was just a couple feet away now.

Ellen stared at the gun. It seemed to wobble in space. She felt dizzy and searched for something to hold onto that could steady her, but there was nothing.

"Ellen?" Scott demanded. He took a step backward.

The gun was farther away now. Could she still reach it? Ellen shook her head in confusion. Had Scott asked her something? His words were all tangled together. Nothing made sense. She squinted her eyes to see better and strained her neck forward to catch what he was saying because she couldn't hear right, either.

"Ellen, look at me!"

What? Wasn't she looking at him already? Ellen closed her eyes tightly and opened them back up carefully. Scott looked so strange to her, so different. Was he taller? Her mind was a puddle of thoughts and emotions.

"Ellen, listen to me. You should believe me that this—" He jerked the gun in his hand to make his point. "—is not about you wanting to play around with Jack Kerwin. You understand that now, don't you?"

Ellen nodded so wildly that it felt like her head might shake loose and float away. Her senses rapidly overtook her reason. She had no idea what Scott might do next, and she didn't know what she was going to do, either. Possible outcomes filled the space between them like a complex web. Ellen squinted to try to see them more plainly.

"Ellen, come back inside for a minute. I just want to ask you a few questions." His voice made her feel like she had swallowed something oily and foul-tasting. Nevertheless, her feet moved forward as if controlled by marionette strings. In a stupor, she followed him back into the apartment.

Scott pointed the gun at a nearby chair. "Sit down."

With movement devoid of will, she walked to the chair and perched on its edge, her body not yet committed to sitting. It still might jump up and run at any moment. The thudding of her heart echoed with each passing second. A cacophony of conflicting information smothered her ability to think. It was like one of those dreams in which she made the decision to run, but her body wouldn't obey.

Scott sat on the bed across from her with his gun obstinately pointed in her direction. He was steady, so different from how she felt. She vaguely noticed his demeanor, a mixture of arousal and disinterest. He was physically excited, yet another part of him looked like a spoiled child unhappy with this year's birthday gift.

These potent perceptions pierced through the fog in which Ellen was trapped. The terror of the animal within her took over as meaning became clear. In an endorphin-fueled rush, she scrambled toward the door. Only instinct controlled her now. One of her heels slipped across the marble, and her legs gave out. She tumbled to the floor only a couple of yards away from him.

Scott leaped from the bed and stood over her. Ellen began to sob, as she lay sprawled beneath him.

"Ellen, I only wanted to talk. You're making too much of this. I wanted you to be comfortable. I wanted you to have a nice, comfortable seat over there." Scott pointed toward the chair she had run from. "But now look what you've done. I guess I'll have to ask you my questions right here." He brought another hand to the gun and adjusted it so it was pointed directly at her heart. He said smugly, "You won't try to move again, will you? I definitely don't advise it."

Ellen knew Scott was talking to her. She wasn't sure why she couldn't hear him clearly. All she could register was the sound of her own sobbing. Her cries echoed in her ears.

She should try to do something, her rational mind advised. But her limbs still wouldn't listen. Some part of her knew she was in shock. She tried to forcibly rein in her emotions.

"Ellen, you haven't answered me. You keep on ignoring my questions, and I don't like that." He forced her flat on her back with his left hand while he held the gun on her with his right. "You're being a very bad servant, not listening to your master. If you're not careful, you will have to be punished." He straddled her and sat astride her pelvis. His arousal announced itself with pressing hardness. The dawning reality of what was happening pressed with the same intensity on her and cleared her mind somehow.

Ellen thrashed to get out from beneath him. Scott used the gun and the strength he had gained from his adrenaline to push her back down. "Stay, Ellen. You're going to answer my questions. Right now."

Ellen lay frozen, shivering. Was that a marble floor beneath her back, or a solid block of ice? Lying there, Ellen decided she would answer his questions to buy time. If she were here long enough, Jack would grow suspicious and come looking for her. With harmonic resonance, that thought connected with another more empowering one. All she had to do was keep Scott here for as long as possible. It was simple.

If he'd wanted to kill her right away, he already would have. Maybe he didn't even want to have to kill her at all. Each encouraging thought called to the next and made a chain of hope that became stronger and stronger. Soon Ellen calmed her heart rate, and Scott's weight no longer felt so heavy upon her.

He seemed to sense her diminishing fear, and it made him mad. He crushed his pelvis against hers and placed the muzzle of the gun under her chin, using it to force her head back. She no longer could look at him. "So Ellen, first of all, why did you want to come here tonight?"

With her neck straining backward, she answered in a choked voice, "I wanted to see you."

Scott twisted the muzzle of the gun deeper. She felt her skin pinch.

"That isn't the truth. We both know that. I don't like it when you lie to me." He moved the gun one inch lower on her neck. It pressed into her throat, making it difficult for her to breathe. "Tell me the truth. You still think I'm stupid, Ellen? I've always known when you've lied to me."

Scott jammed the gun against her trachea until Ellen coughed violently. She couldn't get enough air.

"I've only let you *think* you were getting away with it," he continued. "You're not getting away with it anymore. Answer my question. Answer my question, or I'm going to kill you right now." His eyes shrunk to two minuscule dots. "You think I'm afraid to kill you?" He cocked the gun as if to prove he wasn't afraid in the least.

Ellen drew in a quick breath. Maybe the easiest way to stall was to distract him with the truth—or at least some of it. She didn't dare lift her head to look at him. He didn't seem to like her looking at him. Instead, she strained her eyes in his direction until she could just see him. She spoke with a calm voice that was eerie in its stillness, even to her. "I know you're not afraid to kill me. I know you could kill me right now if you wanted to."

Her response pleased him. Ellen could tell because the pressure on her throat lessened. Of course, she realized, Scott always felt more in control when he was feared. That was what he liked.

She forced her voice into a more tremulous register. "Please, please don't kill me. I'll do anything you want, Scott. Anything!"

The tension in his muscles eased further. He even smiled slightly. "I just want the truth, Ellen. Tell me the real reason why you're here."

Scott relaxed the gun enough to let her neck return to a more normal position. But he still held the weapon uncomfortably close to her face. Her body shivered as she remembered the photos she'd seen in Scott's office that day, the ones she had never told Jack about because they were too terrible to describe. But they were the reason she had to help. "I wanted to find out more about how Tabula Rasa operates."

Scott lifted the corners of his mouth. His false smile made him look even more frightening to her, like the Joker from Batman, whose smile had been cut into his face.

"You know you could have asked me about them anytime, Ellen. I would have told you everything you wanted to know. It didn't have to come to this." He tapped the gun against her throat. The gesture was almost playful, like a cat toying with its prey before devouring it.

"But ... I ... ahh." Ellen stalled. What was more treacherous—a lie or the truth? Ellen took a deep breath.

Scott noticed her inhalation and didn't seem to like it. Did he suspect she was stalling? Once again he pushed the muzzle of the gun down on her throat, screwing it into her as deeply. He almost strangled her. Her breath was ragged and gasping.

He commanded, "Tell. Me. The. Truth."

The pressure on her throat was intense. Ellen forced the lie out between gasps. "I know the Tabula Rasa members are never seen, and it made me curious. I wanted to see if you would take me to see one of them."

His eyes sparkled with pleasure. "We're going to take a little field trip."

CHAPTER 37

DEAD WOMAN WALKING

Jack sped through the corridors at an unnatural pace but he couldn't escape the doubts that pursued him. With each step, self-admonishments battered him like the boxer's fists.

Maxwell's apartment door was wide open. Jack tore through the entrance. It was empty. *Damn.* What had he done? And what had he allowed Ellen to do? He ran both hands through his hair, digging his fingernails deep into the back of his head.

Ellen thought this must be what it was like for a death-row inmate walking to the execution chamber. Time slowed. The end was near, and there was nothing she could do about it. Did those inmates feel like she did—strangely, frighteningly calm? She had already figured out that Scott wouldn't let her live once she saw what he had done to the members of Tabula Rasa. She knew they were no longer human. The photos had made that obvious. She didn't want to see them in person.

She wasn't sure Scott realized he'd have to kill her. But she knew it was her inevitable end. He wouldn't allow his terrible secret to get into the open. Somewhere inside themselves, even monsters like Dr. Maxwell knew the world would condemn them even though they secretly coveted approval. Ellen thought it was a strange, twisted desire. Perhaps, their equivalent of a self-preservation instinct.

Closing her eyes, she conjured the image of her father. She'd somehow become the person she wanted to be, someone like him. As she walked through the dimly lit corridors leading to the TR center, she glanced down at the gold and snakeskin cuff on her wrist, the very same bracelet she'd likened to a shield several hours ago. It hadn't protected her like she had imagined it might, but that didn't matter. Its bold delineations of black and gold still empowered her with their stark statement of presence and purity.

Ellen may not have lived all of her life as a person she could admire, but she could at least greet her death with grace and dignity and her own sense of power. One tiny thread of hope did remain. As Scott had taken her here, she had found a way to leave a trail for Jack. Perhaps it was the angel of her father helping her along the way. She hoped her lover would be able to follow the path and free her from Scott and his madness.

The apartment's hollow space was a testimony to Jack's bad decision-making and to his selfishness. If Maxwell killed Ellen, he would be as much to blame as the mad doctor. He scanned the scene for clues, registering a crimson color that contrasted with the white of the marble floor. Closer investigation revealed it was blood. Probably Ellen's.

Jack gasped for air. He hadn't been this terrified since—he pulled in a strangled breath—since he'd known that Jeremy was going to die. He didn't want to relive that experience, that helplessness. God, had Scott killed her already?

Reason interjected, telling him there wasn't enough blood on the floor to account for a fatal wound. Maybe she'd bled enough to leave a trail. With that plan in mind, he went back into the hallway to search for more bloodstains. It was a gruesome task and one that held little satisfaction.

Crouching down outside the apartment's doorway, Jack peered at the floor for the evidence he sought. A glimmering object pierced his scrutiny. As he reached to pick it up, he saw it was an amber hairpin. Amber, just like Ellen's hair. He raised his eyebrows, alarmed but excited. It might be a meaningless coincidence. The hairpin could have fallen out accidentally. Jack continued down the hallway with wary confidence, praying for another shining pin to guide him.

He had just accepted that the pin had fallen out inadvertently when he saw one right in front of a nearby door as if pointing the way to go. He exhaled a pent-up breath he hadn't realized he'd been holding in and punched 1011 into the keypad. The door popped open. *Hold on, Ellen*, he whispered into the empty hallway.

Ellen grasped the hairpin so firmly it hurt her palm. If she were lucky, this would also be the last door she needed to point out for Jack. She had been lucky so far. Scott had been so enthralled by the thought of showing her his personal horror chamber that he hadn't noticed the way she stalled at each door. The times he did glance back at her to make sure she was following, he failed to notice her hair gradually tumbling out of her tight bun. Ellen was glad for his single-mindedness because it left him oblivious to all else. She was also frightened for the same reason. What did he want so desperately to show her?

Unconsciously, Ellen slowed down. She had always known Scott was a cruel and petty person. Tonight she saw that he was a true psychopath.

Scott turned and shouted, "Ellen, come on! Speed up! Just one more door to go through. Don't you dare slow down now. This is your field trip, Ellen. Remember, you asked for this." Glee bubbled through his anger.

Ellen gulped. One more door. How was she going to deal with that? She had run out of pins. Desperately, she unclasped the cuff on her wrist and held it behind her back as they neared the entrance. Ellen could see the isolated chambers beyond it. They looked like something out of a science fiction movie.

The sterile, dimly lit rooms were depressing. Although they looked mostly empty, they contained strange electronic equipment, devices she had never seen before. She caught the silhouettes of ghostly figures moving within some of the chambers. She clutched an arm around her ribcage to suppress the shiver that played over her skin.

Scott entered the code into the keypad nearest them. At the same time, Ellen dropped the bracelet. She tried to shove it forward with her foot.

He heard the bracelet hit the floor and looked over to see her trying to push it behind her with her shoe. He kicked it aside, and Ellen blanched as it rolled away. Then Scott slammed the door shut behind them. The sound reverberated down the dim hallway.

"You won't be able to escape me, Ellen. You shouldn't even try. Now let's start the tour." He flashed his Joker's smile. "Do you want to see the babies first?" he asked. Then he pushed her hard. "Come on, you don't want to miss all the fun!"

Jack accelerated with the discovery of each pin. There were a few times he had to retrace his steps to go back for one he'd missed, but his progress was swift. All the while, he wished he'd asked Ellen to make a map of the center while they were scheming so he could try to figure out where Scott might be taking her. It had been idiotic not to ask. He clearly didn't think right when he was around her.

Sweat poured down his back as he sprinted onward. He had to get to Ellen before Maxwell did anything worse to her than he already had. Jack knew for a fact that Maxwell owned a gun.

Where was that next pin? As Jack searched for it, he saw the door to the security center that Ellen had described to him. Even though he was desperate to get to her, it might help them both if he shut down the surveillance and security first. She'd mentioned it would only take five minutes. He punched in the code and ran inside. Jack could hardly believe what he saw on the screens. *What a sick, sick man.* Forcing himself to focus, Jack got to the appropriate terminal and followed the instructions Ellen had given him. In a few minutes, all the screens were blank.

CHAPTER 38

IN THE ZONE

Nick was halfway through his peanut butter and jelly sandwich when Melissa got another text from Natalie. "What does it say?"

The lines in Melissa's forehead deepened. "It isn't safe to stay here anymore. We have to get out now."

"Predictable." He stuffed the rest of the sandwich in his mouth, talking and chewing at the same time. "Come down to the storeroom with me. We'll get what we need and get out of here."

Melissa nodded. "Okay."

As Nick walked behind her, he could see her knees wobbling. She was nervous, but he didn't comment on it. Saying something would make her more anxious.

He collected what he needed from the shelves as Melissa held the black bag open for him. He dumped the equipment inside. "Mel, there's something you need to know about me."

She observed him sidelong. "What?" She sounded like she didn't want any surprises, as if her nerves couldn't handle anything else.

"When I go on a mission, or whatever you want to call it—when I do what I need to do tonight—I sort of become a different person."

"What do you mean?"

"I don't know. I call it going into the zone. I become super-focused. But what that really means is that I can't pay attention to anything or anyone else that falls outside the task at hand."

"Oh, you mean like when you don't want me to talk to you because you're concentrating on something?"

"Sort of but worse." He looked at her apologetically. "Sorry, Mel. I've been doing this sort of thing for a long time. It's just how I do it."

"Do whatever you need to. I don't care. Just bring Sidney home."

Nick squinted at the rear-view mirror again. He was pretty sure they were being followed. "Hang on," he warned Melissa, and she clutched the armrest tightly. He swerved into the right-hand lane, and Melissa yelped as her body ricocheted from the force. "Sorry."

"It's okay."

Nick stayed in his lane, keeping his eyes on the mirror until they were at the street he wanted. He turned sharply.

"Nick, this is a one-way!"

"I know!" he screamed back as he maneuvered around the oncoming traffic. He evaluated quickly. *Right, then a quick left. An underground parking garage they could hang out in for a few minutes.* He looked into the rear-view again. He seemed to have lost them. But he went to the garage anyway, just to be certain.

Melissa didn't look his way as they waited. She seemed afraid to talk as if she would knock him out of the zone. Nick considered starting a conversation to soothe her but decided against it. It was probably better this way.

When they'd waited long enough, he pulled back into the street. He drove for one block before he saw the car again. *Jesus Christ!*

"We're still being followed?"

Nick clenched his jaw and nodded. "Hold on!" He jammed down on the accelerator, weaving in and out of cars and running a couple of stoplights until he felt like he had finally lost them.

A couple of blocks later, he saw the car again.

It got closer. Nick veered to the right, hoping to take the next exit. He wasn't fast enough, watching as the exit passed by like an uncashed check. He had to be better. He couldn't afford to be rusty. The car was still behind them, and it was getting closer. He waited and looked for the right opportunity. It wasn't too close yet, but his options were narrowing. Soon there would be none left.

Right. Left. Right. Faster. Turn. Go. Turn again. Pause. Run the light. Quick, into that parking lot. Wait. Wait. Almost. Wait some more. It's okay, I think. It's okay. I lost them.

Nick looked around. Yes, he'd lost them. But now that they knew his car, they would find him again, and it wouldn't take much effort. Time to ditch the car. "Melissa, we have to get rid of this car and take the Metro. You have to be ready to do exactly what I tell you to do, and you can't hesitate." He gave her a pointed look. "Or argue with me."

Her face was whiter than chalk. "You aren't going to get any arguments from me. I can't believe you did this sort of thing for a living. I'm scared out of my mind, and I can't think straight. How do you do it?"

He gave her a half-hearted smile. "I'm an adrenaline junkie, baby." He raised his eyebrows, as if to say, didn't you already know that?

Melissa nodded slowly. "Ah, yes, roller coasters, motorcycles, skydiving, shark tanks, surfing in Hawaii in high season. It all makes sense now."

"I never kept it a secret," he said while speeding frantically down another street.

"No, I just get it now."

"Good. Now hold on again. Things might get interesting."

Melissa gripped the edges of her seat. "Bring it on." The confidence was forced, but Nick appreciated her nerve. He reached over to squeeze her knee, and when she looked up at him, he saw the naked faith in her expression. In that moment, he knew that she was worth everything.

"I'm going to get us to the silver line at East Falls Church. The ride is going to be fast and maybe a little scary, so be ready. When we get there, I want you to run toward the Metro entrance. Don't worry if I'm behind you or not. Just go. Take the first train to Stadium-Armory and wait for me there if I'm not with you already. I promise I'll be behind you."

"Okay."

He dropped her off at the corner, and she ran ahead of him. He couldn't find any place to park. Bad luck. Parking spaces were usually his thing. Now he wouldn't be able to reach her before the subway train came. She'd better wait like he told her. She said she'd learned her lesson, and he wanted it to be true, except there wasn't a lot of evidence to support it.

He threw the keys behind the wheel of the Explorer for the last time and ran to the East Falls entrance. The cold wind breezed through his hair and energized him, making him feel a confidence that probably wasn't warranted given his time out of the game.

Pulling his Metro pass out of his wallet, he slipped the card through the slot and passed through the turnstile. He waited for the train, looking right and left for potential enemies. None. When the train came a minute later, he maneuvered through the crowd. Soon he heading to Stadium-Armory. Nick scanned the car. No one looked suspicious, but he didn't stop searching. It was impossible to know where the threat would come from.

The ride was smooth and uneventful, a nice reprieve. Nick got off at Stadium-Armory, praying Melissa would be waiting there. He rode up the escalator, his eyes alert for possible danger, but again there was nothing. That made him edgy. He wasn't used to things being this easy. It was sort of like the law of statistics: things would even out eventually, and he had to be prepared for that moment.

Nick got outside and surveyed the area for Melissa, not finding her. He was taller than most men, so he tried to stay in obvious places where she'd see him before he found her. After fifteen minutes passed, he started to get worried.

"Hey, Nick!" Melissa swept around his shoulder.

"Where were you?"

"Ladies room. Sorry. It couldn't wait. Were you worried?"

"Yes. I was. I don't think we've been followed, but stay close. Just do whatever I do, and be ready to listen to my orders in an instant."

CHAPTER 39

EINSTEIN'S NIGHTMARE

S cott forced Ellen in front of the darkened one-way glass, making her look. They were in the part of the facility he termed "the Nursery." The name was a grotesque farce. The opposite of the sun-filled nurseries parents prepared for their loved little ones. These infants were unwell and appallingly pale. Their eyes bulged—perhaps an adaptation to the dismal light. Each infant lived isolated in his or her chamber in this underground region of CIRAS.

"Aren't they allowed to play with one another?" She reached her fingertips toward the glass, but Scott slapped them away.

"Don't touch that."

Ellen interlocked her shaking hands and held them clutched to her chest.

"Each of the subjects must be raised in isolation. In this way, they can be properly taught. The computers and training programs are both their toys and their teachers. They are the best, most effective teaching tools ever created." He radiated pleasure, but the upturned corners of his lips revealed the pure evil in his heart.

He gestured proudly toward the futuristic-looking stations in the cells. Everything precisely placed. As Ellen moved past a cell, she saw one of the infants trying to put a geometric object into a lit-up grid. Scott approached the glass to investigate, seeming interested in the outcome.

Ellen could not contain her horror. "They're really always alone?" If she survived, she would need to know exactly what Scott had done to these children. The information might be able to help the children later when they were rescued. The idea of their salvation became a lifeline.

Scott turned and pressed the gun into her ribcage, making it hard for her to concentrate on what he was saying. "Our research has indicated, without a shred of doubt, that they learn best this way." He grinned in that terrible way again, then plowed on, unencumbered by conscience. "With our training, by the time they're thirteen to eighteen years old, they're the best-trained superhuman computers in the world."

His pride was obvious, like a bloodstain on a white shirt. He took satisfaction from these sickly, tortured creatures, like a proud father. Ellen felt nauseated. "They're just babies. How do you take care of them? Who feeds them? Changes their diapers?"

Dr. Maxwell's eyes brightened. "Let me show you. That was one of my more brilliant ideas."

Ellen watched him with disgust. It was hard to believe that he was a human being. She could tell he wanted her to be impressed. What was wrong with him?

Scott continued on enthusiastically, not seeing her aversion. "If they were allowed to interact with other humans, it might interfere with their ability to evaluate information unemotionally. That just wouldn't do. That component is critical to being an effective Tabula Rasa member. So let me show you what I came up with." He started to walk in the opposite direction and waved her over with his gun. "Come over here, Ellen."

Ellen forced herself to move. Her feet felt like blocks of granite, her entire body weighted down by her heavy heart. She kept her eyes on the floor as they entered the region of the TR Center that housed very young babies and toddlers one to three years old.

"See, Ellen?" When Scott saw that she wasn't looking, he jammed the muzzle of the gun under her left cheekbone and brought her face upright. "Pay attention."

He took the gun away, and Ellen inhaled a strained breath as her heartbeat hurtled in her eardrums.

The area was hexagon-shaped, so she was able to see almost all of the chambers at once. The creatures inside, which hardly looked human, were alone and occupied with the computer interfaces in their cells. The light of the devices cast an eerie glow over their already alien-like faces. Many of them were thin, with bones that stuck out at harsh angles. The few that still retained the round faces of normal babies looked even more freakish, with their unnaturally white skin and bulging eyes.

"Walk this way."

Ellen trailed behind him miserably. She couldn't stop the flow of tears as she was forced to acknowledge that these miserable creatures had once been babies who could have laughed and smiled like any others. Pain pulled at her heart, but she stayed as silent and discreet as she could. She didn't want to provoke Scott again.

He stopped her in front of a cell that she hadn't noticed before. "Here."

There was another figure in the chamber with the baby. The individual was clothed head-to-toe in a silver bodysuit made of some kind of stretchy material. Ellen could tell by the shape of the figure that she was a woman, although the material covered every inch of her skin including her face. Her movements were mechanical as she changed the infant's diaper. Coupled with the silver color of the bodysuit, she looked more like a robot than a human.

Scott used his gun as a pointer. "Another one of my perfect solutions. These women who come in to feed, change, and clothe the infants are well trained to offer no stimulation, no motherly love. It's absolutely ideal."

Even during their youngest years, the children given to the Tabula Rasa project had never felt any love or affection once they were brought here. And Scott seemed to be saying that they weren't even allowed to see the face of another human. How utterly cruel.

Could it really matter so much to the project that they had no normal human interaction? Their only relationships were with the computers and programs designed to make them smarter—the smartest human beings that ever existed. How could that be worth it? And where did they get the babies? She should try to find out by keeping him talking. "How can it be good that they receive no affection?"

"Oh, Ellen, it's very good. Because again, research, research! That is the thing! It didn't start off this way, but we soon learned." Scott puckered his lips in distaste and snorted breath through his nose. "Well, I soon learned. That stupid coward Jameson never supported my brilliant insights. But I found a way around that. Bribery has its perks. Anyway, back to your question. I found out that our subjects learned quickest without the distraction of human interface."

Ellen looked at him. She had suspected as much but couldn't hide the horror etched into her expression, obvious as the color of her eyes and the shape of her lips.

"Oh, I see." Scott frowned. "I see you don't believe me," he said, misinterpreting her horror as derision.

The silver woman finished changing the child's diaper and exited the room. No sooner had she left than the child crawled over to one of the interactive learning stations. "Look there," Scott explained as the infant played. "I discovered after several years of trial and error that the infants would attach better to their training devices if they had no humans in their environment. Attachment of any kind interferes with objective reasoning."

"You keep them down here their entire lives? Away from the air, the sun?" She pressed her hand against her mouth, her eyes wide. "How do they survive?"

"Oh, they survive well enough." Scott smiled at the infant who was at the very beginning stages of the TR training program, acting like an adoring parent. It was abhorrent.

He twirled away from the window, looking like he'd just remembered something. "At least, they survive as long as we need them to. Well, most of them." He paused. "They all do their best work when they're young, anyway." He shrugged and walked away. "Come, Ellen. There's more to show you."

Ellen was stunned into silence. She had known since she saw the photos that the TR Center was both a prison and a type of torture chamber for its members. Even so, it was a shock to see it in front of her. She found it incredibly pitiable to see these infants tormented for the sake of scientific advancement. If she survived the night, the image of their wretched faces and pasty limbs would be forever scorched into her mind and heart.

Unwittingly, Ellen whimpered and trembled. The darkness, their faces, the unnatural glow of the machines and computers spun about her consciousness. She shut her eyes tightly to block out the ghoulish figures that demanded attention.

Scott pushed her, and she swayed sideways. "Ellen, open your eyes!" he demanded, his voice tremulous and annoyed. It seemed to frustrate him that she couldn't see the greatness of his creation.

Ellen didn't want to look at them anymore. "I can't. Don't make me." She was interrupted by his fierce grip on her arm. Scott squeezed harder until the skin under his grip turned several shades paler.

"Please!" Ellen begged. She tried to pull her arm away, but she had no strength left. She stood with her arm dangling in Scott's fist as if she were one of the hopeless TR prisoners. Her control broke simultaneously with her will, and she started sobbing again.

"Stop it, Ellen. And open your damn eyes." Scott flung her arm away, and she wobbled backward.

Ellen's body shook while she forced her eyes open. She could feel mascara and black kohl eyeliner dripping down her face, mixed with tears. She couldn't stop her gushing tears, despite the tiny voice in her mind that begged her to, knowing it would enrage Scott and put her in further danger.

"Stop crying, damn it!" He pointed his gun at her with enhanced vigor.

Ellen's tears were like the tremors of the ground before an earthquake. Destruction was coming, and there was no way to stop it. Those sad beings, distorted as they were, were much like she had been for years, strangely twisted by her training. She wept for them and for the years she had lost by not facing the truth about herself sooner and changing for the better.

Ellen couldn't stop her tears, but with the small amount of strength she had left, she compelled herself to stand up tall and face Scott. She would challenge him one last time with whatever dignity she could muster.

She straightened her back once again. That singular motion made her feel transformed into a beautiful, wild creature of streaking black tears, red hair, soul-deep pain, and newborn strength. Barely born, but breathing lustily.

CHAPTER 40

FRACTIONS TOO LATE

Jack rushed out of the security center, running down the corridor in search of Ellen's trail. Nothing. He hurried in a different direction, and there ahead he saw something shiny on the floor.

When he got closer, he saw it wasn't a pin. It was Ellen's python bracelet. He picked it up, his chest heaving as he tried to catch his breath. He placed his hand on the door. This was the last one. If he'd effectively disabled the security, he wouldn't need to enter the code. Cautiously he pulled on the door to test it. A sigh of relief escaped his lungs when the door opened without resistance or the sound of alarms.

He passed through the entrance to the TR Center and was assaulted by the sound of terrible sobbing He raced toward its source, trying to ignore the visions of the macabre laboratory surrounding him. What he saw gave him chills.

As he neared the crying sound, he detected voices woven between the sobs, realizing they belonged to Dr. Maxwell and Ellen. Jack bolted toward them, staggering into the scene then stopped short.

The image hovered in space, as if they were all in stasis together and unaffected by the passage of time. Ellen looked magnificent and beautiful. Her hair streamed riotously around her. Rivulets of diluted black stained her face. Although tears spilled recklessly from some source deep within her, she looked powerful.

Jack shifted his focus to Maxwell. The present seemed to jerk violently and unfreeze. The singular sound of a bullet escaping from a barrel rang brutally into the air simultaneously with Ellen's terrified scream. Her body thudded to the floor.

Jack leaped at Maxwell. "You animal!" he spat. No words could describe Maxwell's evil. Jack ripped the gun from his grasp, aiming it at Scott's head. "I should kill you right here."

Maxwell sniveled incoherently, white with terror. If it were possible, Jack might have thought he regretted shooting Ellen. Jack peered into his disgusting, perverted little face. "I'll deal with you later," slamming the gun into the side of Maxwell's head, creating a nasty gash. The blow knocked him out instantly.

Jack turned to Ellen. He fought to remain calm as he noticed how still she was. Willing himself to focus, he confirmed his fear. Ellen had been shot in the head. This was no accident. Maxwell had been going for the kill. As Jack stared in shock at Ellen's unresponsive features, he knew the doctor had been successful. A pool of blood spread around Ellen's head. Jack didn't want to see any more. He averted his gaze and checked her pulse to confirm what was already obvious. Ellen was dead.

His anger seethed, calm and potent. He looked back over at Maxwell's inert but living body. It was unfair that this monster was the one still alive. Jack contemplated his options. Killing him wouldn't be the best way to avenge Ellen's death, although Jack was strongly tempted to do just that. He thought hard, setting aside his emotions.

Maxwell had used the birthday of CIRAS for all his security codes, despite the fact that it was an easy one to crack. Jack knew what to do next. The one thing that would be better than murdering Maxwell would be to kill the only thing he cared about—CIRAS. And that was exactly what Ellen would have wanted him to do. It was what they had planned on doing together. Jack fought back a sob.

Setting aside his anger and sadness, he saw that one of the nearby cells was empty, the door slightly ajar. A fitting prison for Maxwell. He picked up the gun, shoving it into his waistband, disgusted that it was the one that had killed Ellen. But he had to be practical. He might need it later.

Jack dragged Maxwell by his ankles into the peculiar cell. He didn't want to acknowledge that the members of the TR group working on his project were kept in a depressing place just like this one. They were probably as deformed and distressingly pale as the younger ones here. There was no reason to believe they had turned out differently.

He dropped Maxwell's feet in disgust, stepping out of the chamber, and banging the door shut. As he returned to Ellen, his emotions were a twisted ball of lead that sank deeper into his chest with every breath. He needed to get her out of this awful place.

He lifted her body up and over his shoulder. Now, instead of colliding with his in lust and desperation, her cold form pressed against him. The incongruity of it numbed him. He felt guilty that he was thankful for his lack of sensation.

Her body became colder and more rigid as he made his way back to his apartment, her weight seeming to increase the longer he carried her. As her body hung heavier on him, so did the reality of her death.

Jack entered the large room and carefully laid her body on the bed. He gently arranged her hair and clothing, dampened a towel with warm water, and washed her face of the blood and streaked makeup as best he could. He avoided looking at the large wound on the side of her head.

He was aware these were meaningless gestures, knowing he did them for himself and not for her. There was nothing he could do for her anymore. All that remained was what he should have done. He walked away from her body, recognizing with surrendering calm that he would never be able to walk away from his guilt.

There was no time to mourn her. He'd have to go back down to the basement and take photographs. Then he had to concentrate on getting them to the right person. After that, the process of shutting down CIRAS could begin.

But first, he needed to help Elvis evacuate the other residents.

Jack pounded his fist against Elvis's door. It opened, and Jack's hand hung in space. He unclenched his fist and let it swing to his side.

"Jack?" Elvis greeted him. "What the ..." He moved out of the way, and Jack surged into the room. "There's blood all over your shirt! Are you hurt?"

"The blood isn't mine."

"Whose ... ?"

Jack closed his eyes and swallowed. "Ellen's. Maxwell killed her."

"Oh my God." Elvis's gaze lifted off Jack and zoomed around the apartment. "Where is he now?"

"He's unconscious. I knocked him out and put him in one of the TR cells." Jack pulled his hand through his hair. "I don't know if it's safe for us to stay at CIRAS. The cameras are down, but somebody will get suspicious and will come here to check it out. And whoever they are, they probably won't see things from our point of view. Come with me and help me get the other residents out of here. You should take them to the Metro station and get as far away as you can."

"Okay." He stared at the stains on Jack's shirt. "Want a shirt?"

Jack glanced down at his blood-soaked Oxford. "Yeah, thanks." He started to unbutton it. "Can I use your bathroom for a minute?"

"Of course. It's in the same place as in your apartment. I'll get you a shirt."

Jack turned on the water and let it run until it was hot and steaming. Closing his eyes, he thought of Ellen. She hadn't even had a chance. He pumped the soap into his palm and lathered his hands, arms, and chest. There was blood on his chin and neck, too, so he scrubbed those. Pink water swirled down into the drain as he rinsed off.

When he emerged from the bathroom, Elvis handed him a T-shirt. "It's probably too small for you, but..."

Jack didn't let him finish. "Thanks." He reached for the shirt and pulled it over his head. Somehow it felt wrong to be washed and clean. The blood was gone, but it didn't change the fact that Ellen was dead.

"What do you need me to do?"

"Do you know where the other apartments are?"

"Yeah."

"Take me there. They don't deserve my help when they wouldn't give me theirs. But I don't need them on my conscience, too."

"Let's go." Elvis stuck his hands in his pockets and walked out the door as Jack followed behind.

The other apartments weren't far. Elvis headed to Rachel Woo's first. She opened the door and gawked at them.

Jack asked, "Can we come in?"

"Why?"

Jack stepped into the room. "You need to leave CIRAS," he told her, not wanting to explain it all.

Woo laughed. "Leave CIRAS? I don't think so." She looked at him like she thought he was insane. "Sorry, but I can't remember your name," she added with a bite in her voice and pushed the door to close it.

Jack's reflexes were quick. He shot out his hand to stop the door from smashing into him. "You might be in danger."

She rolled her eyes.

Elvis said, "Look, he's right. Scott Maxwell killed Ellen Standis."

"I don't see how that proves I'm in danger."

Jack threw his hands up. "Then you're insane, and I shouldn't bother helping you. But you should know I'm getting this cursed center shut down, so you won't be able to stay here for long."

"You can't. Not yet. I'm so close."

Jack spat his next words. "You're close? You're close? A woman has been killed tonight. Do you get that, Dr. Woo?"

Jack could tell by her confused expression that she didn't get it. She just wanted to go on with her research until the world fell down around her. He felt ready to explode.

He tried to explain it to her again. "A woman has been murdered. A woman who worked here, just like you. The man who runs this hellhole shot her! You know him—Scott Maxwell. He sent you your invitation to come here. You remember, don't you?" He used his stare like a javelin, trying to force the truth into her. Woo remained cold and unresponsive, unleashing his temper. "You know what? Stay here. Be my guest. I hope your research works out for you, you cold, heartless bitch!"

Jack spun around, catching Elvis's attention. "Come on."

Woo stared blankly ahead, then looked up at them as if she had just noticed they were there. "No, wait. I'll come with you."

"Fine, come on, then," Jack said and stalked down the hall to the apartment of Dr. Chaudri while the other two followed behind.

Chaudri was not as immovable as Rachel Woo. Once he found out Ellen had been murdered, he was more than willing to leave. For that, Jack was grateful. He gave them directions to the Metro station and sent them off with Elvis.

CHAPTER 41

RESCUE?

"We'll head toward Anacostia Park," Nick explained. "CIRAS is nearby. It should go okay unless we're being followed. If we are, that's when I'll rely on you to act quickly. You promise you'll do what I say?" He was being repetitive, but he still didn't quite trust Melissa on that account.

"I will."

"Let's go. We'll walk briskly but stay nonchalant. We're just business people heading home after a late day at work."

"Got it." Melissa walked away from him at a swift pace.

Nick ran to catch up with her. "We need to cross Independence Avenue, over here." Nick pointed.

"Okay."

"Now!"

No one followed them. Too much good luck, and Nick didn't like it. Bad was bound to follow soon enough.

"I see it just behind those trees," Melissa said after a few minutes.

"That's it. Hang on. Come over here with me." Nick dashed behind one of the larger trees. Melissa copied his movement. "Mel, make out with me, quick."

"What?"

"Just do it. Now."

Melissa wrapped her hands around the back of his neck and started kissing him. Nick watched the couple walk by. After they passed, he slid the black bag off his shoulder and brought it into the narrow space between their bodies. He felt around inside until he found the right shape and pulled it out.

"What's that?" Melissa asked through the side of her mouth.

Nick put the small device into his inside pocket. He held his face close to Melissa's. "Blocks security feeds for a short time. Comes across on monitors as a natural disruption." He turned away from her and shifted the bag to his back. She started to move, too. "Wait. Stay there."

Melissa checked her next step and stopped.

"Now reach into the bag but stay really close and make sure no one sees. Get the Glock and slip it under my jacket and into my waistband."

He heard her fumbling. The gun felt cold as it touched his skin. "Let's go. We'll head right to CIRAS and figure out where you can wait for me once we get inside."

"Can't I just go with you?"

"No, And, I need you to stop asking questions. We're wasting time."

She looked down. "I'm just worried about Sidney, you know, after what Warner said about him. It sounded like they were thinking of killing him." Her voice shook.

"We'll get Sidney out as soon as we can. I'm sure he's fine. Warner was just trying to scare you."

"But—"

Nick shot her a stern glance. Emotions had to be put aside. There would be enough time to deal with them later.

Melissa swallowed hard. "Okay. I trust you. Just tell me what to do." She got a curious look on her face and put her hand into her pocket.

"Did you get a text?"

She nodded, looking down as she walked. "Mmm-hmm. It's from Natalie: 'Someone disabled the security at CIRAS. No one has noticed yet, but they will soon and then they will go there. Don't know how much time you'll have.'"

"At least we don't have to worry about shutting down the security. That's one good thing." He picked up his pace.

Melissa hurried beside him. "Suppose they get to you before you have a chance to get out of there."

Nick thought of his luck balance. "Nothing I'll be able to do about that."

"Is that supposed to make me feel better?"

"There's no time for feelings right now, Mel. We have to act. I can only control what I can control. Now come on." He started to jog, and so did she.

The large glass doors loomed before them. "How the hell do we get in?" Melissa asked. "I can't see any kind of handle."

"There isn't one." Nick searched through the black bag.

Melissa stared at him. "Jesus, is everything in that bag?"

"Almost." He rummaged around some more. "Found it." He produced a small switchblade and flicked it open. "Watch." He slipped the blade through a crack between the two panes of glass.

"Really?"

The door slid open. "Only because the security is down. Come on in." As he spoke, he put away the knife and snatched the Glock from his waistband. He held it close as they went inside together.

"Where is everyone?"

Nick had to admit it was unnervingly still. "No idea." He scanned around for someplace where Melissa could wait for him. He felt her staring at him. He shifted his gaze to her. "What?"

She blinked rapidly. All her muscles looked like they were tensed up. "I can't wait here alone. I'll be too scared. It'll drive me crazy."

"And you can't come with me. I don't know what's down there. I won't put you at risk."

"Suppose I come with you but wait outside the center?"

Nick considered her suggestion. It might be a decent compromise. "You promise to wait outside?"

She nodded. "It'll be easier for me than waiting here alone."

"Okay. Stay close and quiet."

Melissa nodded.

"I don't know exactly where I'm going, so you'll just have to follow my lead. I'll figure it out."

"I know you will." Melissa quivered and clutched her sides.

Nick thought it must be hard for her to be in the place where her son was being held captive. She probably wanted to run right to him.

He looked at her again and clutched his weapon tighter. He angled toward the nearest wall, searching for an exit to the foyer, but couldn't find one. The walls appeared seamless, even though he knew they couldn't be.

He walked the perimeter, looking for evidence of an opening. He didn't find anything, so he walked around again. This time he let his fingertips graze along the wall. He felt a slight ridge.

There. He passed it again. There it was. No doubt. He eased the crack with his knife. The wall opened up. He heard Melissa gasp behind him, but he didn't stop to look at her. He headed straight down the long hallway.

TR would be in the basement. That was the most secure, most secret place there. The security system was down.

Doors. This one on the left? No, that's an apartment or something. Looks like a hotel room. Try that one. Same. Go to a new area. Try over to the right. New hallway. Lots of curved walls. Makes sense. The outside is curved, too. Try this door. Another hallway. Good. Keep going. Long hallway. Where is the next door? Here, in front, hallway ends. Keypads are at every door. but security's down. Hall swerves to left. Door on right. Open it. Stairs. Good.

Nick took a deep breath and brought the gun close up in front of him. He sensed Melissa's chest constricting behind him.

Step down. Quietly. Reach the landing. Another set of stairs. Be more careful. Quieter. They could be expecting you. Control your breath. Control your mind. Steady. Easy.

No more stairs. Last door. This must be it.

He turned around. "Stay here."

"Here?" she asked in a shaky voice. She sounded disoriented.

"Or go back and wait somewhere upstairs. You can't come with me."

Melissa glanced at him and then at the stairs. "I'll go back."

They were wasting time. Nick pivoted away from her and opened the door.

CHAPTER 42

PARALLEL FORCES

Fresh blood covered the floor. Nick cocked his gun, checking the area for suspicious activity. Silence. Whatever had happened it was over now. He put the Glock away and took the small video camera from his jacket pocket.

He walked through the bowels of CIRAS, recording everything as he passed through the twisted labyrinth. The humans who'd been trapped underground for years were grotesque and distorted. Their appearance made Nick feel sick to his stomach. He hated himself for thinking that they were disgusting, but they were.

Sidney was one of these things. Nick was relieved he didn't know which one was Melissa's child because he was already feeling guilty about the way he felt. Thank god Melissa wasn't with him.

Though their bodies were clearly unhealthy, when Nick began to think about the emotional damage Sidney and these others must have suffered, he wanted to punch someone—or something. Even the walls were tempting him to strike. "How could they do this?" he screamed. His voice echoed back, sounding feeble and inept. Maxwell's center was worse than the prisoner experiment Warner had sanctioned.

Nick felt dirty recording this human misery on film, but it was required. He held back his thoughts and continued on to another cell. There was something different in this one. *Holy Christ!* Maxwell was in there. There was no way he could forget that face. Somebody must have dragged him into the cell. Nick tried the door, and it opened. He stepped closer, pulling his gun out.

"Get away from him," a voice yelled from behind.

What the hell? Nick turned to see a tall man pointing a gun at him. Although the man had an athletic build, Nick could tell he wasn't skilled with a gun because he didn't hold it right.

The man said, "Put your gun on the floor, or I'll shoot."

Nick paused. The man stepped closer, his eyes ablaze with fear and something else Nick couldn't place. "Tell me who you are."

"Not until you put that gun down."

Nick cocked his gun and pointed at the man. "You put yours down first, and I'll consider it."

The man hesitated.

"Unless you're sure you're a more accurate shot than I am."

His gun wobbled as the guy clenched it so hard his knuckles turned white.

Now Nick was sure he wasn't a threat. "Look, I'm guessing we're on the same side. Just tell me who you are. I won't shoot."

"Jack Kerwin. I'm—um, I was—a resident here."

"What are you doing down here?"

Jack's eyes flicked downward. He yelled, "Watch out behind you!"

Nick spun around. Maxwell was up, and he had a Ruger LC9 in his hands. He must have had it somewhere on him. He aimed it at Nick's head. "Where's Ellen?"

"Who?"

Jack screamed at Maxwell, "You bastard! She's dead!"

Maxwell looked bewildered. "Dead?"

Nick interjected, "I don't know who or what you two are talking about, but Dr. Maxwell, I want you to put that gun down now, or I'll shoot."

Maxwell grinned wickedly. "Oh, really?" He fired at Nick.

Nick heard the bullet pass by his ear as he fired back. Maxwell fell back onto the floor.

Jack ran toward Nick. "Are you okay?"

Nick rubbed his ear. "Yeah, he just missed me. Close call. I'm Nick Sperry." He shifted his gun to his left hand and stuck out his right. "Guess we are on the same side."

Jack shook his hand. His palm felt sweaty. "Guess so."

Together, they moved over to Maxwell, who was bleeding profusely from the base of his neck. Nick knelt beside him and put a forefinger on his wrist. "No pulse. Can't say I care."

"No, me neither. He deserved it."

Melissa skidded into the room behind Jack.

"Melissa, what the hell—" Nick started to say.

"Nick, you have to come quick, now!" She tugged at his arm.

Nick wasn't sure she even registered Maxwell's dead body on the floor behind him. "Hey, hold on. Tell me what happened."

She took a few rapid breaths. "Okay, well, I went upstairs like you said, and I didn't want to wait for you out in the open, so I went into one of the rooms in that hallway that had a lot of apartments in it. And, Nick, there was a dead woman on the bed."

"Ellen?" Nick asked, glancing at Jack.

"Ellen."

"You know her?" Melissa asked Jack.

"I knew her." He looked at the floor.

Melissa asked, "What happened?"

"Dr. Maxwell murdered her."

Melissa stared down at Maxwell's body. "If anyone ever deserved to die that man did."

"As much as anyone ever has." He turned to Jack. "I've recorded everything down here on video."

"That's what I came back down here to do."

"Good. You make another recording then we'll upload both of them and you can take yours straight to the nearest network. We can't let anyone get away with this."

"No, we can't." Jack agreed. Jack pulled out his phone and started filming.

Nick heard Melissa sobbing. She'd walked away while he talked to Jack. He followed the sounds. When he found her, her face was pressed against the glass of one of the chambers. Inside was a child who was probably Sidney's age. He could have been her missing son.

She asked, "How do we know which one is him?"

Nick wrapped an arm around her and felt how cold she was. "We don't, not yet. But we'll be able to find out. I'm sure there are records."

She strained her eyes toward him. "Can't we just let them all out now?"

Nick enfolded both arms around her. "Mel, we can't."

"Why not?" Sobbing, she burrowed her face into his chest.

He stroked her hair. "It might not be safe for them. This is all they've ever known, Mel. We have to do what's best for them. For Sidney."

Melissa sighed. "I know. It's just tearing me to pieces inside that I'm this close, and I can't have him back."

"We'll get him back, Mel." That just made her sob harder.

Nick saw the flashing lights first. There were about ten cop cars congregated around the front entrance.

Melissa asked, "How can we get out?"

"There's got to be another exit."

"How about by a cafeteria or something like that? They would need to have a way to bring in food, and people would have to be able to get out if there was a kitchen fire or something."

"I saw one on the map. This way."

They rounded a turn and a large, glass-enclosed courtyard filled their view. "This is it." He walked close to one of the glass walls, and it opened automatically.

Mel stepped through. "Which way now?"

Nick thought he saw a way out in the opposite direction and pointed.

Without responding, his girlfriend sprinted toward the place he'd pointed at. When Nick finally caught up with her, he said, "Didn't know you could run like that."

"Adrenaline." She nodded toward the café's entrance. "Let's see what we have."

They ran through the seating area and into the kitchen. "Over there," Melissa called. "The exit sign."

CHAPTER 43

RADIO NOWHERE

J ack hurtled out of the Metro station, the drum of his heart thundering in his ears. He squinted and oriented himself, trying to block out the percussive beat. He found the direction of WKSB and headed that way. The video had to get out beyond social media and onto the networks. Now. He considered it his life insurance.

He bolted into the building. Less than a dozen feet away, a young, pretty brunette sat at a desk. She raised her eyebrows, and he realized how ragged him must look.

"Can I help you?"

"I have breaking news. You need to get it on the air." He knew he sounded like a crazy person.

The woman raised one perfect eyebrow. "Regarding?"

"CIRAS."

She pursed her lips at him. "One moment, please. Sit over there." She lifted her hand in a frustratingly casual and condescending way, gesturing toward a group of chairs to her right.

"I think I'll stand." He crossed his arms and waited. The back of his neck prickled with fear.

"If you prefer." She picked up the phone and said, "Yeah, there's a guy here who says he has some breaking news about CIRAS ... Okay ... Okay, I'll tell him." She regarded Jack. "They said to tell you to wait in the seating area." She pointed to the chairs she had shown him before. "Over there." She pointed again. "In case you were wondering." She flashed a quick, false smile.

He waited. Standing. The receptionist kept on glancing up as if to see if he was still there. When he caught her eye, she smirked. The woman was stepping on his very last nerve. Wasn't she supposed to be friendly? Didn't they want to be the first one to break a story? They did. They should. Wait a minute. How long had he been here?

He glanced at his phone. Fifteen minutes. Too long. All of a sudden, everything snapped into a clear picture. Energy tingled through his limbs and into his stomach, where it stayed and started to turn to acid.

"I can't stay any longer," he told the brunette. Before she could reply, he walked out the door with fast strides. So much for his life insurance.

Outside, Jack started to run. Even though it was a cold night and he wore only Elvis's T-shirt and jeans, sweat cascaded out of his pores. His perspiration chilled immediately when it met the air.

He ran a couple of blocks, heading in the general direction of the Metro when he saw flashing lights up ahead. He reoriented to the right to avoid them. It seemed like more popped up whichever way he turned. He couldn't be sure he was the target, but it sure felt like it.

Ducking into an alleyway on his immediate right, he waited there to catch his breath. He pulled out his phone, punched a few keys, and posted the video on five different social media sites. There. He should have done that first.

Jack crept out of the alleyway. He felt exhausted, the weight of his limbs doubled. Stopping must have drained his adrenaline. There were glimpses of red and blue lights in every direction he looked, and he wouldn't be able to get past all of them. The only alternative was to walk right by. Maybe if he tried to look casual, they wouldn't notice.

Jack coursed briskly down the street. As he neared a Metro entrance, a group of cops emerged. One of them ran toward him and held out a badge shouting, "Jack Kerwin, you're under arrest..."

There was only a second for Jack to decide what to do. Fight or flight. Or give in. Jack sprinted in the opposite direction, willing his legs to go faster as he fled around the corner.

Glancing over his shoulder, he noticed that his pursuers had fallen back. He broke a quick left and pumped his arms hard. His legs flew. He ran past several blocks without thinking. It felt like those last few minutes of a soccer match when the score was tied, and it was imperative to make a crucial play.

Jack placed his foot down on the curb of the next block and chanced another look backward. They were even further away. Thank God. He slowed his pace and turned forward.

Damn. There was a whole new set of cops in front of him. He had nowhere to go. Jack blinked rapidly as if that would change reality. It didn't.

A different one held out his badge. He and three others approached. There were no alternatives. He held his hands up in a pose he'd only ever seen in the movies.

"Jack Kerwin, you are under arrest for the murder of Ellen Standis." He positioned himself behind Jack to handcuff him and was ready to restrain him if necessary. Jack's mouth gaped open. He was too shocked to resist.

The cop continued. "Anything you say can and will be used against you in a court of law ..." They read him the rest of the Miranda rights,

"I didn't murder her. Dr. Scott Maxwell did. I was trying to rescue her. I can prove it."

"That's what they all say," the police officer replied with a laugh in his voice. He looked over at one of his colleagues so he could share in the joke, too. They sniggered together.

Jack clenched his teeth in a firm line. The tendons in his neck rose up in tight cords that continued to the collar of his shirt. His body was alert and ready for action, but his brain knew there was nothing he could do.

A different officer said, "Don't think we don't know that could be part of your cover. Make it seem like you were the good guy, when you were the one who murdered her all along. It's more common than you think. None of us were born yesterday." The guy had a Boston accent.

Jack's words flew from his mouth without forethought. "Jesus Christ, is the whole damn city in bed with CIRAS? Do you even know what they do there? Do you have any f'ing idea? Do you guys have children?"

The police officer looked at Jack like he was deranged. "Just trying to solve a murder, sir." The corners of his mouth lifted, but his eyes were hard. "Please come with us."

Jack pressed his palms together, which made the cuffs press into his wrists. "I want to call my lawyer."

"You will be allowed counsel," the officer said. "Now, Dr. Kerwin, let's go." The one who spoke gave him a rough push.

Jack glared back at the offender and had to exercise extreme control not to give him a hard whack in the balls. *So much for trying to do the right thing,* Jack thought. *Nobody around here gives a crap.* "Jesus Christ," he muttered, and continued to swear under his breath as they pushed him into the car. He looked out the window, remembering his first day at CIRAS. Who would have known it would come to this?

Someone forced Jack into the room with an unnecessary shove. The lighting was miserably low, so he couldn't see much. His hands were still cuffed behind him, which made him feel doubly vulnerable. In defiance, he raised his chin and looked around. He refused to appear defeated.

The room was dingy and dirty. It was so depressing that it must have been intentional. There was no place to sit. He was sure that was also planned. They wanted to break him down. *So don't let them get to you*, he thought.

In the center of the room was a solitary table. Jack looked back at the man behind him, who shrugged. Something in his eyes hinted of guilt. "I suggest you just wait," the man said. He left the room and locked the door behind him.

Jack stood and waited until his friend and attorney Jimmy Hudson walked in. Jimmy gave Jack an emotional hug, which actually scared him a little, because Jimmy wasn't exactly the hugging type.

His friend stepped away, giving him a rough slap on the shoulder. "Hey, I'd say it's good to see you, but ..." He smiled with only half his mouth.

Jack finished his sentence. "But under the circumstances, not so much. Yeah, I guess I understand." He cocked his head to the side. "So can you get me out of here?"

Jimmy frowned and didn't answer immediately. "Jesus, what did you get yourself into?" He wheeled his head around to locate some place to sit.

"No chairs."

"They want to make you uncomfortable, huh?"

"Yeah, I think so." Jack looked around the horrible room and then back at Jimmy. "But I have to admit I'm already pretty uncomfortable. I'm being accused of murdering a woman I cared about. I wanted to save her. I tried to ..." Jack's gaze fell to the floor.

"They say your prints are on the gun, Jack."

"I explained that to them."

"Okay, now explain it to me."

Jack described how things had occurred.

"I know you're telling me the truth, but you have to understand they have another way of looking at it."

"Which is?"

Jimmy swallowed. "They say that you killed Ellen, and Dr. Maxwell tried to stop you. After that, you knocked Maxwell unconscious and locked him up in that cell."

"Where did they get that load of shit?" Jack attempted to lean on the table. It tilted sharply, "Damn it!" he yelled, glaring at the unstable piece of furniture as if it were the source of all his problems. Without thinking, he punched it hard with his bound fists. No sooner had he done it than he realized it had been a very stupid idea. He shook his hands to try to reduce the painful stinging sensation in his knuckles.

"What did that table do to you?" Jimmy tried to joke. When Jack didn't even break a smile, he said, "That's Maxwell's side of the story."

"He's a dirty little prick!"

Jimmy looked at him seriously. "Your prints are on the gun, Jack."

CHAPTER 44

A MOTHER'S LOVE

N ick approached the exit. "I'll go first."

Melissa nodded with her lips pressed firmly together.

He got out the Glock and pushed the door open. Keeping his right shoulder against the door, he crouched down and peeked around the edge of the door. "It's clear. Go!"

Nick bolted. Melissa was right next to him."Straight?" she asked.

"Yes, to that group of trees over there."

They dashed to the clump of poplars, hunkering down behind them. Nick asked, "See that small building over there?"

Melissa followed the direction he pointed. "Yeah."

"Aim for that. Then send that video out as soon as you can. It might be the only thing that keeps me out of jail."

"And gets Sidney out of CIRAS."

"Yes." Nick wondered if Mel thought he was being selfish, but the reality was that he had shot one man and killed another. If there wasn't good evidence that showed why he'd done those things, he would be serving jail time and a lot of it. "Are you ready?"

"Yes."

They dashed to the building. It was some sort of storage unit, by the look of it. They sat with their backs against the wall, parallel to CIRAS. Melissa was breathing heavily. Nick pulled the video camera from his pocket. "You ready to do your thing?" Being younger, she knew how to do this crap better than he did.

Melissa nodded, attaching a cord from the camera to the phone. She started to type. Nick got up and looked around the corner of the building to see if anyone was coming. After a couple minutes, Melissa called out, "It's sent."

"You got all of them? The national ones, too?"

"Yes, all of them. And every social media site, I could think of." Her face was tight. Nick knew why. She didn't have Sidney back yet. The only thing that mattered to her.

"Let's get out of here."

"Please tell me it will work."

He picked up her hand and clasped it between both of his. "Yes. Yes, it will." He felt one of her tears drop onto the flesh of his thumb. "We need to leave here, Mel. Now. You still trust me?"

"Yes." She rose up.

Her voice sounded tired, although she was trying not to show it. She had been through too much tonight. He needed to get her some rest, but home wouldn't be safe. Nowhere might be safe. But a hotel would be better. He had thrown a couple of Sam's IDs in the bag. A wave of sadness flashed through Nick as he thought of Sam, but he parried it aside. He had to concentrate.

His thoughts obediently lined up in a row: a small hotel would be better, and they should get there as soon as possible. Close to CIRAS was fine; no one would suspect that. There were a lot of surveillance cameras in D.C., so they shouldn't get on the Metro again. They would be spotted too quickly. Walking was best.

He asked, "Can you find us a small hotel near here?"

She brought her phone out of her coat. "I think so." She started moving her finger around on the screen. "Nothing is that close." She toggled around some more with her fingertip. "Everything is across the river. There's a C Street Inn about two miles away that has a vacancy. But do you want to walk across the bridge?" She looked at him to decide.

Nick had limited choices, and he didn't like it. Still, a decision had to be made. "Let's call a cab."

"That's best?"

"How the hell do I know?" He knew Melissa could sense his indecision. "But we can't stay here. I do know that."

Melissa grabbed his hand. Nick interpreted it as a vote of confidence.

Melissa's phone vibrated. She looked at Nick. "Should I answer it?"

"See who it is first."

She looked down at the screen and bit her lower lip. "It's Victoria."

Nick's expression softened. "She's probably worried about you. You should let her know you're okay."

"Hey, Vic," Melissa said. She paused. "No, we're fine. Nick is taking care of me." She offered him a faint smile. "Sidney? No, we have to leave him there for now. Nick says it might not be safe for him to leave yet." Another slight smile. "Thank you. Nick will watch out for us. I'll try to call you tomorrow. Love you."

She looked back up at Nick. "I should probably call that cab now."

"You need to get some sleep," Nick said gently as Melissa paced back and forth in their room at the C Street Inn. They'd had no trouble getting to the motel and checking in, but the danger was far from over. He knew her endorphins and concerns about Sidney were keeping her awake.

She plopped down into a chair. "I know I should be exhausted, but I feel so wired."

He poured a glass of water and fished a couple Xanax out of his wallet, handing them to her.

"I can't take those. I'm too worried."

"Mel, you have to. If you're deliriously tired, you won't be able to be there for Sidney when he needs you."

She downed them. In five minutes, she was out.

Sunlight made a long, bright line between the heavy drapes. Nick must not have pulled them completely closed the night before. A slim rectangle of morning draped over him and Melissa as they lay in bed. She rolled over and pressed her body close to his, laying a hand across his abdomen. She wasn't quite awake but would be soon.

Nick waited, alert for several minutes before he slipped out from beneath Melissa's embrace. She groaned and turned over but didn't wake. He walked over to a chair where her coat hung, taking her phone from the inside pocket and going into the bathroom.

He entered *CIRAS* into the search engine. The results populated, and they were all about the Tabula Rasa scandal. He felt his shoulders sag in relief. *Thank God.* It had worked. He had good news to tell Melissa when she woke. He read the story quickly, noting the most important details.

"Nick?"

"I'll be there in a second, honey." He shut off her phone and met her in bed.

"Is it over?"

"Yes. Authorities have already evacuated everyone from CIRAS."

Veins popped out on her temples. "The Tabula Rasa group, too?"

"Yes."

Melissa reeled out of bed so swiftly that Nick was worried she might faint. "We have to go to him,"

"He's been taken to a local hospital along with the others. A group of social workers and psychiatrists has volunteered to determine the safest way to integrate them into the real world."

"We have to find out where Sidney was taken. I need to see him."

"Not yet. They're keeping him in isolation like everyone else. They pulled all their records from Sunshine and are going to start contacting relatives."

Melissa fell back on the bed. "When?"

Nick sat beside her. "You have to have faith, Melissa."

"In what? In who?" Her face looked empty, blank.

"In your love for him."

CHAPTER 45

INCOMPLETE REDEMPTION

J ack sat on the thin, filthy cot. It reminded him of the bedrooms in his fraternity at Harvard. It was disgusting.

He had already sent out the video. He was positive of that, even though his memory felt shaky. That evidence should help him get exonerated, shouldn't it? The alternatives weren't worth thinking about.

He guessed he should be thankful they had put him in a single cell. Jack wasn't sure if the rumors about prison life were true or not, but he sure didn't want to find out.

The problem was there was too much time—time to think, regret, mourn. Things were easier when he had to move, decide, and take action. This was much, much worse. There was no urgency to help him push aside the image of Ellen's dead body.

When he heard the sound of the door opening, Jack lifted his head. It felt heavy, hard to move.

"You're free to go," Jimmy Hudson said as he and the sheriff approached Jack's cell.

Jack jumped up from his cot. "What changed?"

"I'll explain once we get you out of here," said Jimmy.

It would feel good to be a free man again. His thoughts flashed toward the trapped beings of the TR Center. Were they free now, too? He hoped so. It felt awful to be caged.

Once they were alone in Jimmy's car, his friend explained all that had transpired in the past seventy-two hours. The footage of the TR Center had been played on the news for the whole world to see. And the whole world was definitely watching. It was all anyone was talking about.

Jimmy filled in the rest. "Maxwell bribed Warner years ago to take on the CIRAS Tabula Rasa project. It was an offer Warner couldn't refuse because the doctor offered him an outrageous bribe. Maxwell had the money—trust fund kid, you know. Jameson never knew anything about it. And since Warner was interested in making more money than the NIH would ever pay him, he started looking for other ways to profit from his relationship with Maxwell. Ultimately, Warner cultivated a bribery ring between himself, certain members of the CIA, and the clients of the Mafia. Nobody else knew about it until just a few days ago."

"But that doesn't fully explain why they let me go. I mean, I'm kind of the one who brought everyone's precious research center crashing to the ground. They could have kept me in jail just for the hell of it."

"Well, the US government is in a deep load of shit now, and they don't want to be. Maybe they think they can't trudge out of it no matter how high their wading boots are." He paused. "Also, they did an autopsy on Ellen's body." Jack winced at his words, and Jimmy looked apologetic.

"Sorry. Anyway, they found out that because of the angle of the bullet wound, someone much shorter than you must have shot the gun."

"Someone Maxwell's height."

"Exactly."

SILVER LININGS

"Don't feel guilty, Jack." Nick patted him on the shoulder as they gazed across Anacostia Park in the direction of the CIRAS building.

Jack took in a slight breath. "I don't think the guilt will ever go away."

"The cure is going to save lives."

Jack turned to face him. "But what about the lives that were sacrificed? Sometimes I think I should have left the TR notes in that knapsack under the bed." He averted his gaze.

"And what good would that have done anyone?"

Jack was silent for a few seconds. He sighed. "None, I guess."

"That's right. None. You have to try to focus on the positive side."

"It seems awful that there even is a positive side."

"I know. But there is. Melissa and I approve. Don't beat yourself up."

"I'll try."

Melissa sat with Tanya Nadella, Sidney's psychiatrist, in her cheery, sunlit office. Although she sometimes enjoyed the bright light from the large windows, there were other times when it hadn't seemed appropriate to sit in such a sunny setting. But today the light wasn't such a sharp contrast to the way she felt. The words Tanya had shared with her shimmered with hope.

"Are you saying he'll be normal?"

"No, not exactly."

Melissa's shoulders slumped.

"I'm afraid none of them will ever be normal." She paused. "But Sidney is special, I think. I'm sure some part of him has known love, however long ago it was. He has a natural resilience that not all are blessed with. He..."

She stopped again, and Melissa could see that she had altered what she was going to say. "You're both very lucky. Sidney will never be quite normal, as you and I look at it. But, I think he will be okay."

Melissa was almost afraid to believe what this woman was telling her. If it weren't true, it would hurt too much. The past few months had already been so hard for her, and for Nick. "Are you sure?"

"As sure as I can be. It will take work. There are things you'll need to do. And it will definitely take time. I'm afraid it will take lots of time. Time, love, and patience."

Melissa shook her head as if shaking away the idea that it would be any trouble at all. Nick had taught her how much love could overcome and overlook. "I'll do anything I need to. Everything I need to." Melissa laughed and sniffed through happy tears. "Would it be okay to see Sidney today?"

She wasn't allowed to see him every time she came, and sometimes when she did, it was only for a few moments. Sidney didn't quite understand that she was his mother. He had been taught what the word meant but didn't have the context for processing the meaning of it yet. Miraculously, he appeared to take great pleasure in simply holding her hand. Sometimes that was what they did for hours on end as they walked around the facility's playground area. He still had to wear special sunglasses and clothing to protect him from the sun. But he had lost some of his unhealthy pallor and had gained some weight. He seemed to enjoy being outside.

"Yes, I think that would be fine. Let's go to him now."

They walked side by side to Sidney's room, which also had a large picture window that looked out on the property. It, too, had a protective shield to keep too much light from entering. The doctors said that in time, his body might adapt, but for now, these measures were needed. As they entered, Sidney turned to look at Melissa.

She looked back at her son and smiled brightly. "Hi, Sidney." Her body vibrated with exuberance for the future they might have together.

In response, he moved his mouth in odd contortions. Melissa wasn't quite sure what he was trying to do. Then one of his attempts flashed into an expression she had seen thousands upon thousands of times before, and she gasped, shocked into silence. Eventually, she found her words. "Sidney... Sidney, I think you're trying to smile."

Not caring whether it was the right or the wrong thing to do, she ran to him. She enclosed her arms around her child, embracing him in a deep hug, and wept.

It broke her heart with the tender pain of a mother's love when he raised his weak arms and laid them across her shoulders in his best imitation of a hug. Melissa lifted her gaze and saw Nick watching the two of them, his tear-glazed eyes matching hers. She waved him over, and together they encircled Sidney in their arms.